One minute remaining . . .

There were still about ten kilos of Pentanex left in the bomb – enough to blow him to smithereens – but Felix could see the whole circuit now. It was a standard timer circuit. He allowed himself a smile. He was safe to cut out the battery. Felix pulled his 'snips' – his wire-cutters – from his assault vest and leaned in to position the jaws either side of the battery's two connecting cables. He could almost feel the crisp clunk as they cut the thick-wound strands, his favourite sensation. This one's in the bag! The bomb is dead . . .

He allowed himself a look of satisfaction. Finished.

But some sudden instinct made Felix open his eyes . . .

D0308674

www.**tripwirebooks**.co.uk

Also available by Steve Cole:

Z.Rex

Also available by Chris Hunter for adult readers:

Eight Lives Down

Extreme Risk

TRIPWIRE

BY STEVE COLE

AND

CHRIS HUNTER
BOMB-DISPOSAL EXPERT

CORGI BOOKS

TRIPWIRE
A CORGI BOOK 978 0 552 56083 2

First published in Great Britain by Corgi Books,
an imprint of Random House Children's Books,
A Random House Group Company

This edition published 2010

1 3 5 7 9 10 8 6 4 2

The Random House Group Limited supports The Forest Stewardship
Council (FSC), the leading international forest certification organisation.
All our titles that are printed on Greenpeace approved FSC certified
paper carry the FSC logo. Our paper procurement policy can be found at
www.rbooks.co.uk/environment

Set in 11/14pt Frutiger by
Falcon Oast Graphic Art Ltd.

Corgi Books are published by Random House Children's Books,
61–63 Uxbridge Road, London W5 5SA

www.kidsatrandomhouse.co.uk
www.rbooks.co.uk

Addresses for companies within The Random House Group Limited can
be found at: www.randomhouse.co.uk/offices.htm

THE RANDOM HOUSE GROUP Limited Reg. No. 954009

A CIP catalogue record for this book is available from the British Library.

Printed and bound in Great Britain by CPI Bookmarque, Croydon, CR0 4TD

The Minos Chapter is a wing of the Anti-Terrorist Logistics Assessment Service. Its recruits, drawn from the armed forces of 15 countries, are rigorously trained in a wide range of specialist skills.

Their mission? To turn terrorist tactics back on the terrorists themselves.

All Minos recruits are teenagers.

All of them operate in top secret.

MINOS OPERATOR PROFILE

FILE: CLASSIFIED
Name: Felix James Smith
Operator Passcode: 1179
Operator Status: Active

Operator Role: Entering battlespaces where the disabling and removal of improvised explosive devices is key

Additional training: Tactics, firearms, physical fitness, advanced driving, covert entry techniques, military freefall parachuting, scuba and closed-circuit diving, boat handling and vehicle hotwiring

Age: 15

Additional information: Father, Aiden Christopher Smith, former ATLAS bomb-disposal operative. Killed in Day Zero attack

CLASSIFIED INFORMATION

MINOS HANDLER PROFILE

FILE: CLASSIFIED
Name: Zane Alexander Samuel
Operator Passcode: 0108
Status: In active ATLAS service

Operator Role: Handler: Liaison officer between Minos recruits and ATLAS

Age: 22

Additional information: Mentor for new wave of recruits, including Mr Felix Smith and Ms Hannah Geffen. American citizen, based internationally

CLASSIFIED INFORMATION

MINOS OPERATOR PROFILE

FILE: CLASSIFIED
Name: Hannah Marie Geffen
Operator Passcode: 7205
Operator Status: Active

Operator Role: Undercover and covert surveillance and observation duties. Specialist linguist.

Additional training: Foreign languages and cultures, undercover surveillance, tactics, firearms, covert entry techniques

Age: 15 (can pass as an older teenager)

Additional information: Of South African origin. Assigned to work with Captain Michael John Sommers, retired SAS

CLASSIFIED INFORMATION

MINOS OPERATOR PROFILE

FILE: CLASSIFIED

Name: Classified (Known Alias: 'The Girl')

Operator Passcode: ATLAS resource number 4286

Operator Status: Active

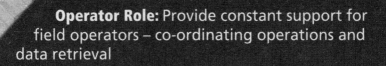

Operator Role: Provide constant support for field operators – co-ordinating operations and data retrieval

Additional training: Strategy, high-speed high-volume data retrieval, tracking skills, high-level computer hacking

Age: 15

Additional information: White female of Eastern European origin. Assigned to ATLAS's shadowy 'Tera-head' department; further info restricted

COUNTDOWN COMMENCING:
... TWENTY-SEVEN ...

Got you.

The sight of the bomb hit Felix like a punch in the guts.

Just twelve minutes remaining on the clock.

Wisps of CS gas hung in the air like ghostly fingers as he inched his way closer. Felix could hear the assault teams clearing the final few rooms around him – bursts of automatic gunfire and the rhythmic thud of the distraction grenades. He tried to tune out the swearing, the shouting, the commands barked out over loudhailers, and focus on staying calm. On doing his job.

The bomb looked ordinary. It could've been an oversized toolbox. Padlocked, of course. There was a digital LED clock on the outside. The numerals shone like laser sights, clustering on his brain.

Felix suddenly realized the building had become eerily

silent, as though the whole place was holding its breath. He could smell his own sweat and the two eyepieces on his S10 were starting to steam up. Again he willed himself to stay calm. A device of this size could wipe out the building and everyone in it in an instant. He was going to have to move fast.

There seemed to be no hidden devices on or around the bomb itself. He unfastened the zip on his assault vest and removed the XPAK explosives detector. He gave its baton a quick swipe over the case.

Pentanex 8, he realized. *Three times more powerful than TNT. If it detonates now we'll be vaporized.* Images crowded into his head as he imagined the outcome of a bomb like this one detonating. *A storm of debris smashing through the surrounding skyscrapers, pounding the vehicles below to scrap. Shards of glass slicing the air. Bodies charred to ash by the high-energy fireball . . .*

There were only ten minutes left on the clock now. Felix felt his body start to shake. *Get it together*, he told himself. *Got to breathe . . . got to focus . . .*

Everything's riding on this.

He took out his hand-entry kit from his bergen – his trusty backpack – and removed two picks. Carefully he worked them into the padlock. As he held the lock's spring-loaded teeth in place with the first pick, he took the pressure of the drum with the other and gave it a sharp clockwise tug. In seconds the padlock was free and the lid of the case was now a little looser – just enough to see if anything had been secreted around the lid. The sweaty seconds went on blinking away. Felix gingerly felt his way along the seal of the case for hidden switches, and as he got to the fourth side he could see the tiny silver bail arm of a micro-switch next to a light sensor.

Felix swore. The bomb was booby-trapped. He was going to have to cut in.

Quickly, precisely, he took out his gas-powered hot-knife – a small pen-like device with a sharp blade heated by a tiny gas cartridge – and made the first incision into the case. Seconds later he cut another, and another, until finally he had a small square hole just big enough to poke his night-vision monocular into.

Inside he could see the bomb's TPU, its timing and power unit: a small circuit board covered in electronic components, complete with detonators, a battery pack and the Pentanex 8, of course – there were maybe 50 kilos of the stuff.

His saliva was like thick paste as he swallowed hard. If he messed up now . . .

Go for the battery pack. Felix could hear his instructor's voice in his mind. *The TPU is the brain of the bomb, but the power source is its heart. Rip it out.*

Seven minutes left . . .

Cutting frantically away with the hot-knife, Felix felt alive, intoxicated with the rush of adrenaline. But there was dread there too, a sick feeling in his stomach. He knew he needed to extend the size of the hole first if he was to stand any chance of tracing the wires to the micro-switch. The noise of the assault teams had died. The only sound he could hear now was the thunder of his heart. Sweat made his black jumpsuit cling clammily to his skin.

Five minutes . . .

'Done it,' he breathed, aware of the sweat pooling at the bottom of his respirator. It wasn't perfect, but the hole was now big enough for Felix to have a dig around. He pushed his night-vision device further into the cavity, looking left and then right, and finally running under one of the packets of Pentanex. He held his breath. There were the two wires leading from the microswitch to the TPU.

We're in business. Felix pulled out a pair of surgical forceps, gripped the first of the wires and attached a probe to its plastic sheath. As he felt it bite into the shiny silver wire inside, something seemed to click inside him. Emotions bled away as almost mechanical action took over. His hands stayed steady as he grasped the second wire and did the same, his focus unfalteringly on the job in hand.

Four minutes . . .

He attached the handheld circuit detector and anxiously waited as it eworked its magic on the micro-switch wires. For a moment he felt a surge of panic. *There's no time*, he thought, *no time for this*. But though he was right up against it, he knew he had to do this the right way.

Cut corners and you cut your own throat.

Felix clocked the reading on the circuit detector. The micro-switch was definitely a trigger. He knew that if he opened the lid he'd be blown to pieces. Already he was deftly removing the two probes so he could get to work on the micro-switch before removing it from the circuit.

Two minutes . . .

Not before time. Now, with the micro-switch out of the equation, he could open the lid and get to the TPU. Felix flicked open the two latches of the pelican case. Blood whammed through his temples as slowly, so slowly, he raised the lid . . .

Nothing.

Now, get it cracked. Your whole life depends on it.

Felix knew that ideally he should remove the battery first. But it was partially obscured by the explosives, and with so little time left it made more sense to separate the explosives from the device instead. He got to work, meticulously cutting away chunks of Pentanex with his ceramic clasp-knife.

One minute remaining . . .

There were still about ten kilos of Pentanex left in the bomb – enough to blow him to smithereens – but Felix could see the whole circuit now. It was a standard timer circuit. He allowed himself a smile. He was safe to cut out the battery. Felix pulled his 'snips' – his wire-cutters – from his assault vest and leaned in to position the jaws either side of the battery's two connecting cables. He could almost feel the crisp clunk as they cut the thick-wound strands, his favourite sensation. *This one's in the bag! The bomb is dead . . .*

He allowed himself a look of satisfaction. *Finished*.

But some sudden instinct made Felix open his eyes.

To find the timer flashing down to zero.

He cried out, nothing coherent, rage and helplessness crushing in as a blinding white light swamped his eyes.

The sound of a blast shook through the room. Felix ripped off his respirator and goggles, shielded his eyes from the sudden burst of floodlights above him and watched a banner unfurl from the ceiling.

BOOM! You have just failed.

COUNTDOWN CONTINUES
...TWENTY-SIX...

'Game over, Smith.'

Felix remained on his knees as the floodlights dimmed, the sound of the simulated explosion still ringing in his ears, adrenaline still churning through his veins and sickness rising in his throat.

In the doorway stood a spook that Felix hadn't seen before. A heavily built man with a face as sharp and smart as his suit. ATLAS, no doubt – or, more formally, the Anti-Terrorist Logistic Assessment Service, set up to implement bold strategies designed to steer the war on terror to a satisfactory conclusion. He was clearly someone high up in the organization too. His hooded eyes guarded the emotions his curled lip gave away.

'Congratulations,' the man offered, his fists clenched. 'You just got one thousand people killed.'

Felix stood up slowly. 'The timer . . .' He found his

voice sounded thin and quiet to his ringing ears. 'The timer was rigged, sir.'

'Oh, really?' The man was staring him out. 'God save us from little kids who think they're men. How old are you now?'

'Fifteen, sir.'

'I've been told you're almost as good with improvised explosive devices as your father, Smith. A born natural. But after your performance here . . .'

'With respect, sir – that timer was definitely rigged.'

'Respect?' The spook looked irritated. 'I wasted manpower and resources on a simulation that's a hair's-breadth away from the real thing because Colonel Kemp told me you show real promise as a candidate for the Minos Chapter.' His fist clenched and unclenched, gave away a glint of metal against the palm. 'This was your chance to shine, Smith, to show ATLAS what you can do under full combat conditions. All you've shown me is a whining brat who can't accept that he's messed up—'

'I didn't mess up, sir,' Felix insisted, his voice trembling a touch now. He yanked the timer from the pelican case and held it up for the spook's scrutiny. 'This has been adapted from a radio-clock – it stays accurate by receiving a time-code signal broadcast from a radio transmitter. Only this one must have picked up a rogue radio signal that caused it to *lose* time. A signal that's most likely coming from that portable transmitter you're holding in your left hand . . . sir.'

The man's eyes gave away nothing.

'I had defeated that bomb when you triggered its

collapse,' Felix went on. 'It wasn't hard acting like the simulation was one hundred per cent real, because my future is on the line here. I'll take any test you've got, a hundred times over. And you can forget the expensive simulations and go with a real bomb – because if I can't make the best of the best right now . . .'

The man's lips finally twitched in a smile. 'Ready to stand up for yourself, whoever's giving you the roasting, eh?' He looked down at his open palm and the miniature transmitter nestling there. 'Yes, you're your father's son all right, aren't you, Smith?'

Felix started, pride kindling in his chest. 'You knew him, sir?'

'I did. Before I joined ATLAS, my background was with the Special Air Service Regiment and subsequently MI6.' He stared at Felix, but seemed to see right through him. 'Your father deployed with us on a number of operations during that time, saved my skin on more than one occasion. Colonel Kemp knew him too. We have high hopes for you, Smith.'

'Then . . . please, sir, won't you let me prove what I can do?' Felix said. 'I need this.'

'And Minos needs the best.' The spook produced a piece of paper, wrapped it round the transmitter, and pressed it into Felix's free hand. 'Take the train to London and report to this address at twenty-hundred hours.'

'Am I in?' Felix asked, his heart banging as the spook turned and walked out through the door as quickly as he'd come. 'Sir, the Minos Chapter . . . am I going to be made an active operator . . . ?'

But the man had gone.

Felix checked the address he'd been given. It was somewhere in Marylebone, north-west London – not a million miles from where he'd grown up in St John's Wood. He felt drained, but he supposed he had a couple of hours or so to rest before he took off. Whatever the meaning of this appointment, he had a feeling that by the end of it, one way or another, his future would be clear.

He picked up his Bergen and let the timer slip to the floor with a clatter. It lay flashing zeros behind its red, scuffed face.

...TWENTY-FIVE...

For Felix, it wasn't much of a walk home. The 'Killing House' training facility where the simulation had taken place had been built in the grounds of Moccas Court, a rambling country pile now transformed into a secret ATLAS training centre in the tranquil Herefordshire countryside.

He walked in a daze through the well-tended grounds. Could it really be almost three months since he'd first arrived on the train out of Paddington? Like the other recruits, he thought at first he'd made it onto the ATLAS fast-track training course for young recruits who'd demonstrated exceptional ability; no mean achievement and something that pretty much guaranteed them an officer's commission in the regular armed forces if they wanted to go career military once they'd turned seventeen. Felix still remembered his thrill at receiving Colonel Kemp's unexpected additional briefing three weeks in, after many recruits had dropped out or been pushed; when the warm-faced old soldier had revealed that they were really here to train for active service in the Minos Chapter. *It's real, then*, he'd realized. *The barrack-room rumours and whispers, they're all true . . .*

Kemp had explained that in Victorian times, kids as young as six were treated the same as adults – they worked long hours, earned a wage, could even be locked up for breaking the law. In more recent times things had moved to the opposite extreme – the nanny state wrapped kids up in cotton wool, trying to protect them from anything the world could chuck at them.

But Day Zero had changed all that. It had changed everything.

The name 'Day Zero' had been coined by the media. But it was more than just an easy shorthand for the destruction of Heathrow Airport and the thousands of lives lost in the greatest terrorist atrocity yet staged. It was as though those few, terrible hours had brought a close to one way of living and birthed another that was colder, harder through necessity.

Now that the minimum age for soldiers on active operations had been lowered from eighteen to seventeen, the school-leaving age had been lowered to fourteen for those wishing to enter the armed forces; young adults could come to the military and learn a proper trade while training to protect their country. And the very best, those who showed exceptional aptitude in different disciplines, they came here, ready to be groomed for greater things.

Ready to be seconded to the Minos Chapter.

Forged in the dark fires of a Britain recovering from its biggest peacetime attack, Minos was a secret wing of the Anti-Terrorist Logistics Assessment Service, itself answerable to GI5 – the Allied Secret Intelligence Service drawn from the special/black ops forces of fifteen countries. An international set-up, its administration was based here in the UK, where Day Zero had cut deepest.

The idea was that teenage operators could get places that their adult counterparts could not. Minos agents could infiltrate radical youth groups and get close to tomorrow's terrorists. They could be used to wrong-foot terrorist opponents on the lookout for adult agents, operating covertly in danger zones without arousing suspicion. Fundamentally, it was turning terrorist tactics back on the terrorists. Time and again terror groups had used innocent kids to help carry out their kill-campaigns.

Now kids like Felix had been trained to pitch hell back to them. 'Unless we can't go the full distance,' he muttered, looking down at the cracks in the paved path as he walked on. 'Unless we fail.'

The training had been full-on and relentless as the hand-picked recruits were taught the so-called 'black art' of being a spy. The sight of each and every building here sent a stack of incredible memories toppling through his mind.

He passed the gymnasium – nicknamed the Slaughter Room by bloodied recruits – where he'd endured endless bouts of brutal close-quarters combat training. More soothing to the memory was the block containing the photographic studios and technical workshops. He passed the laboratories where he'd mixed up his own explosives and the testing range where he'd detonated them, sending a jolt through those in the grand old lecture rooms across the lawn.

His bones ached wearily at the sight of the assault course at the furthermost edge of the west wing; an assortment of four- and five-metre walls, nets and ladders, water-filled tunnels, swinging tightropes and barbed-wire entanglements that stretched out for almost a kilometre through the woodland behind the annex. Beside it, he watched a fresh batch of trainees unleashing a hail of automatic gunfire into the targets on the outdoor rifle ranges.

He watched the new recruits with mixed feelings. *Twelve weeks ago I was like you*, he thought. *Giving it everything, up for the lot. Eager to learn and willing myself to be good enough.* He closed his eyes, savouring a bittersweet rush of memories, good and bad. He and the other recruits had been trained in the tactics and use of all kinds of modern weaponry, from explosive devices to blades and firearms. They'd tackled everything from advanced driving to covert entry techniques, military freefall parachuting to scuba and closed-circuit diving, boat handling to vehicle hotwiring.

Biggest, most awesome ride of my life.

He bunched his fists. *It can't stop here. It just can't.*

The gunfire rattled on. Felix opened his eyes and pressed on towards the common room. Major Fawcett, one of his instructors, strode past in the opposite direction; he saluted automatically and she nodded her head briskly as she passed. 'Good afternoon, Mr Smith.'

It had taken Felix some time to get used to being addressed in the same way that people used to greet his dad. On their first day of training Major Fawcett had explained that while ATLAS had a hierarchy, its members had no rank – and Minos was no different. All new recruits would be referred to as Mr or Miss Whoever, and treated with dignity and respect because that was how they were expected to conduct themselves in turn – as adults.

None of which had stopped Felix from calling the Major 'Steel-Buns Fawcett' behind her back, of course; but then this was the woman who had regularly sent him and his fellow trainees out on fifty-kilometre speed-marches with their Bergens packed full of rocks, up and down wet Welsh mountainsides in the dead of night.

He smiled grimly. If that had all been for nothing . . .

Blisters made lousy keepsakes.

Wondering why he was even trying to laugh off the possible end of all he'd worked for, Felix slouched through the common-room door. The big, oak-panelled space was all but deserted. A big TV fixed to the wall blared away to itself, a news programme showing views of New Heathrow, almost ready for opening – '*a true phoenix of modern architecture,*' the reporter's voice-over reckoned grandly, '*that thanks to unprecedented inter-national co-operation has risen in record time from the bitter ashes of Day Zero – as the shockwaves of that blackest day in modern world history continue to be felt . . .'*

'Gee, do you think?' Felix muttered, looking away automatically. However amazing the new airport looked, he could only ever think of it as a tombstone for all who had died there – his father included. He was glad to see that his roommate, a New Zealander, 'Private' Pete Adams – named not for his rank, but because of the suspicious noises he made under the covers after lights out – was sitting in a chair hunched over his battered DS, working his thumbs over the buttons.

Felix slumped beside him. 'So . . .' He recognized the game's sound effects. '*Tour of Duty Four* again, huh?'

'Yeah. Nice to have a military life you feel some control over.' Pete paused the action and glanced up at him. 'How'd it go with the big training task?'

'Not sure,' Felix admitted. 'Bit of a weird one.' He held out his hands and pretended they were shaking. 'Or do I mean *wired* one?'

'You? You've got the safest hands in England.' Pete paused. 'Which is why I'm glad I'm normally based in Kiwi-land.'

'Ha, ha.' Felix brooded for a while. 'They're sending me someplace in London tonight.'

Pete looked at him sharply. 'Why?'

'No idea. No idea if it's even a good or a bad thing.' He shrugged. 'This headshed showed. Tore into me a bit.'

'Good luck with that, then.' Pete said. 'Course, if I'm honest, I'm *hoping* you failed. Ross too, and Sherman.

'Cause statistically, if you lot fail, that means I stand a higher chance of having passed.'

'Cheers, mate.'

'You're welcome.' Pete grinned, but they both knew he was only half joking. His smile soon faded, and a haunted look glimmered in his dark eyes. 'I know I messed up my final hostage-rescue exercise. Too damn slow.'

'Cautious,' Felix corrected him, remembering the way he'd bricked it during the same exercise a couple of weeks ago. 'Cautious is better than cocksure, yeah?'

'Well anyway, won't hear the verdict till tonight.' Pete shook his head and unpaused his game, returning to the action. 'Why make us wait? Haven't they tortured us enough?'

'Come on, it's a walk in the park round here and you know it.' Felix tried to give him an encouraging smile but it felt nine-tenths grimace; not that Pete noticed anyway, now he was fast-roping from a tactical helicopter with coalition forces. 'And . . . it's not over till it's over, right? We'll have got through. Ross and Sherman too, I bet, even if it's not with straight As.' He nodded. 'You wait. This time tomorrow we'll be partying like there's *no* tomorrow.'

'There really won't be,' said Pete sullenly, 'if we *haven't* got through.'

Silence resumed between them. Felix stared over at the TV and wished he had a real friend here, not just people he'd trained with. But Minos operatives generally worked in isolation, and weren't encouraged to form personal ties. Felix supposed life as an agent was traumatic enough without the fear of losing any more of your nearest and dearest . . .

He became aware that the note of the TV presenter's voice had changed. Felix's attention snapped on like a light; she was talking about a terrorist incident in Chicago. An Improvised Explosive Device had detonated outside a big bank headquartered there. His guts twisted as the screen showed live coverage of the carnage. 'Jeez, not another one,' he breathed. 'When did this kick off?'

'Couple of hours ago,' said Pete. 'Twenty-four dead. God knows how many more wounded.'

'Who's taking credit?'

'Who else? Orpheus.' Pete shook his head and tutted sarcastically. 'It's getting so your old-fashioned terrorist groups can't get a look-in.'

Felix didn't smile. Truth was, since their coup with Day Zero had launched them into the global spotlight, Orpheus operators were perpetrating more and more terror acts worldwide. It was getting so that a week with the death toll in single figures was said to be a triumph.

Now the TV showed a couple of experts dragged in from somewhere or other, whose opinions would fill the dead minutes between updates:

'There have always been those who believe that their objectives can be achieved through acts of violence,' a balding man began. *'Traditionally, terrorist groups have been motivated to act by many things – to draw attention to their cause, or to seek change in their governing conditions, or because they believe their religion demands*

it . . . But now, with the coming of the Orpheus organization, we are seeing a new phenomenon . . . A recognition that isolated pockets of resistance will never overcome an alliance of global powers unless resources are pooled. Orpheus may prove to be just the first of a whole network of terrorist super-groups, where certain of the beliefs of its individual organizations are set to one side so that they may join together and wage a wide-spread war of terror against the West.'

Another pundit, a newspaper editor, spoke up. *'Our only possible response to this constantly escalating threat is to fight back,'* he barked, voice as hard as a hammer. *'We need strong action in place of reaction. This so-called "super-terrorism" must be smashed . . . We've put up with endless debate over the forming of ATLAS and kids joining the army, but the bills got through – now what we need are some results . . .'*

'Working on it,' Pete called to the screen without looking up.

Felix said nothing. He remembered his dad practising a speech he had to make at a military dinner somewhere, delivering the last line in a number of ways, trying to nail the perfect pitch. *In the modern battlespace, anyone can be a victim . . . and anyone can be a combatant.* Felix had joined in, saying the words in silly voices. They'd laughed about it, then, the words losing all meaning as the accents grew dafter; real, till-your-ribs-hurt laughter.

I'll choose combatant over victim every time, Dad. Felix checked his watch, the battered Seamaster that had once belonged to his father. It was close to five. What the hell, he'd sign out now and head to the station. Better to feel he was moving anywhere than just standing still.

He slapped Private Pete on the shoulder. 'Laters, yeah?'

'Let's hope so,' Pete murmured.

Felix hardly heard him, heading for the door and wondering if he'd ever be back.

. . . TWENTY-FOUR . . .

The speeding train's windows showcased about a thousand fields and towns. Staring blankly, his stomach tight with nerves, Felix was reminded of his journey down to Herefordshire to start his training. Back then he'd been scared because he had no idea of what lay ahead; a fear of the unknown. Now he felt he had learned so much, and was simply afraid that he'd never get the chance to show it.

The train pulled into Paddington. The drab estates and blackened industrial architecture were a far cry from the wide-open spaces he'd grown used to around the river Wye. It felt to Felix uncomfortably like a dream of something better had come to an end, and now here he was back where he belonged in the built-up city.

The address was only a couple of miles away, so Felix decided to run the distance. The evening sun was glaring down and his pack weighed a ton but after Steel-Buns Fawcett's little outings it was no bother. He loved running, got a real buzz from exercise. A six-mile wake-up run, twenty minutes of sprinting and an hour in the gym was his daily minimum . . . And after this afternoon's rigged hoax devices and the latest news from Chicago, he badly needed to work off some tension.

Since Day Zero, even before he'd joined the army, he had taken to working out several times a day. More than one counsellor had suggested that this habit was linked to a deep inner need to feel strong and empowered in defiance of circumstances that left him feeling weak and powerless.

Once, Felix reflected, he might have believed there was something in that opinion. But he reckoned now it was more about focus, about reaching the goals you set yourself. And maybe it was just a little about catching fit girls' eyes as he ran past; that was fun, stopped him dwelling on things. And savouring the smiles he received was about as intimate as he was prepared to get with the opposite sex right now. He couldn't afford distractions. ATLAS only took the sharpest and the best.

The Minos Chapter, he thought, pounding over a railway bridge, sweating in the sunshine. The name sounded so grand and mysterious, selected – so Colonel Kemp had explained – in direct response to the terrorists. '*Orpheus*' was derived from old words for 'darkness' and 'to put asunder'; the Orpheus in the old myths was a figure who'd entered into hell and walked out again unscathed. Minos, on the other hand, meant 'king', and was named for the son of Zeus who became a judge of the dead in hell. As well as all that, apparently it was a pun on 'minors', acknowledging the age of its members.

Hilarious, thought Felix, slowing his pace; a group of old people were spilling slowly from a white coach and blocking the pavement. Masking his impatience with a smile, he stopped for them, barely out of breath, and looked about.

Then he frowned. He hadn't been focusing on a particular route, but while his mind had been brooding, his feet had steered him back to his old neighbourhood.

He hadn't been here for a year; not since Auntie Mags had gone ballistic at him for quitting school and joining up, forging her signature to do so. Luckily she had only kicked him out of the house instead of grassing him up. And living away was no great loss – the barracks was warmer, and the cookhouse served better meals. But it was a bittersweet feeling, being back around here.

The High Street hadn't changed so much. Felix remembered hanging out here on Saturdays with his mates, spending what little cash he had in Maplin Electronics; he used to build his own radio-controlled creations while Dad was away on a tour, to impress him when he came back. One time he'd made a miniature PackBot, like the 'wheelbarrow' robots Dad used to clear caves and bunkers of improvised explosive devices. Dad had been so impressed he gave Felix extra cash to make it bigger and better, helping him with the plans. He always said that when it was good enough he'd take it out with him and use it in field ops for real. *He can't have meant it*, Felix supposed. *But back then, I really believed that he would take it, some day. Did more to motivate me than school could ever manage.*

With a fond smile, he walked over to the burger bar his dad had always taken him to following a tour of duty. Through the window he could see a man laughing with his kid, both their straws stuck into the same milkshake. Felix felt a pang of envy for their simple, carefree enjoyment. He remembered so many lunchtimes lasting all afternoon in this place, as Dad talked about his exploits in the field; leaving out the sensitive details, of course, in case the walls – or the suspect-looking burgers – had ears. Iraq, Afghanistan, Colombia . . . The places sounded so exotic, like other worlds.

Felix turned away, remembering their last trip here.

'No more going away for me, mate.' Dad's smile was as solid and strong as the rest of him. *'I'm taking the new intelligence posting with ATLAS.'*

'Result!' Felix had knocked knuckles with him. *'Though Auntie Mags says you've never had intelligence.'*

'She's not your mother's sister for nothing.'

'I told her she was wrong.'

'Whoa! You're a braver man than me, Felix.'

Felix couldn't stop smiling. *'So you'll be around the whole time from now on?'*

'Mostly. I won't be entirely desk-bound. Got to keep my hand in, haven't I?' The crinkles round Dad's eyes deepened with his grin. *'But yeah, I'll be around. Better get used to it, mate.'*

'I never got the chance,' Felix breathed. He realized he

was getting some funny looks from the customers inside, so he turned from the window. 'No time to get used to it.'

Dad had volunteered to go out to Heathrow on Day Zero. He'd been on the trail of bomb-makers with a similar MO to the ones who'd been caught on Terminal Three, and wanted to check things out in person.

'*Don't forget the rules, Dad.*'

'*I know, I know – come back safe.*'

Felix jerked back into a fast run. He remembered little of the numb, dark days of the aftermath. Only two things stuck in his mind, picked over by the shrinks and the counsellors a hundred times afterwards. As he increased his pace in the here and now, he could still hear his Auntie Mags from two years ago, talking on the phone to his mum and her new bloke in Australia; remembered his tears falling onto his fists. '*You knew this would happen some day. After all he put you through you still stood by him. But you were right to get out when you did . . .*'

And he remembered smashing his PackBot to pieces with a baseball bat and screaming up at the still-ashen sky. The first and last time he'd ever really lost it. *Control your aggression*. That was the best lesson the army had taught him. Don't waste your anger – channel it to achieve your objectives.

Felix ran faster and faster, tearing down the bus lane in a desperate, bone-jarring sprint. But the memories were hard to outrun, burning in his head like the stitch in his side.

* * *

When he'd sweated out a few of his demons and cleared his head as much as he could, Felix jogged over to the address he'd been given. For the thousandth time he wondered why the spook had sent him here without a word of explanation. Then his heart sank as he read the name plaque screwed into the fancy porch: DR JENSON, PSYCHIATRIC CONSULTANT. He'd seen enough shrinks in Day Zero's aftermath to last him a lifetime.

Still, there was no turning back now. Felix announced himself over the intercom and was buzzed through the outer door by the doctor himself, full of nerves and fore-boding as he followed a cantilevered staircase up to the first-floor landing and through a set of curved double doors into a long corridor. What was the spooks' thinking in sending him here to a private practice – why not a military shrink? Did ATLAS believe he was so hung up on hitting back at the scum who murdered his dad that he would make an unreliable asset?

He was stirred from his thoughts by the creak of a heavy wooden door opening at the end of the corridor, and the vague smile of a grey-haired, wiry-looking man in glasses welcoming him in. 'I'm Doctor Jenson,' the man announced. 'I have full ATLAS clearance, so we can talk freely. Major Fawcett likes me to have a word with some of her students . . . Would you come through, Felix?'

Here we go. A lump slowly rising at the back of his throat, Felix followed the doctor into his office. In or out, chapter one or game over – it didn't take a genius to know that his whole future depended on what happened next.

... TWENTY-THREE ...

Once Felix had been settled on a couch in the study, Jenson wheeled out a small, squat medical machine. A digital display winked on and off as the shrink applied electrodes inside little pads of plaster to his chest, wrist and temple. Each electrode trailed a thin wire back to the grey plastic box-of-tricks.

'Shock therapy, is it?' Felix joked, trying to act unfussed.

The shrink made steeples with his fingers. 'Tell me about the dream, Felix.'

'I'm a stone's throw away from passing Minos training. I'm living the dream.'

'I mean the dream about your father,' Jenson prompted. There was a pause, which Felix had no intention of filling. 'The dream about Day Zero.'

'Oh, that. Right.' Felix glanced down at the wires

trailing from under his clothes. He could now see that the machine was set up to monitor his vital signs – blood pressure, heart rate, all that stuff. It could function as a lie detector, or it could paint a graphic picture of his emotional response to anything the shrink asked him.

Felix knew why he was here.

'I don't have that dream so much any more,' he said, stretching out on the couch. *And I've done enough raking over old bones for one day.* 'My dad was killed – end of. I worked through it with therapists before I joined up.'

'I know. I just would like you to tell me the dream.'

Felix rolled over onto his side, fiddled with one of the wires. 'All right. I used to dream I was watching my dad defuse the Improvised Explosive Devices at Terminal Three.'

'Go on.'

He took a couple of deep breaths, tried to sound bored. 'I'm down on the Heathrow Express platform. You know what happened.'

'But I would like you to tell me.'

Felix nodded wearily. 'The whole deal, huh?'

'Everything.'

'OK. Well, it's really just like it happened in real life. I start off knowing that a man tried to detonate a suicide bomb on the train. It didn't go off.' Felix kept his tone neutral. 'No one was harmed. Bomber was apprehended but he'd left another IED on the train and a suspect package was found on the platform. The area was cleared in a hundred-metre radius – standard procedure. Closed down the whole train line. But evacuating the airport wasn't considered necessary – that platform's a good ten minutes from the airport.'

'Of course,' Jenson agreed in his most understanding, trustworthy voice.

'Plus there were no suspect packages reported above ground and armed guards were patrolling all terminals,' Felix went on. 'For all the good it did.'

'For you to go over these actual facts at the start of the dream' – Jenson leaned back in his chair – 'it suggests that a part of you wonders if your father could have insisted to his superiors on a full evacuation of the airport and so dramatically lowered the death toll.'

Felix bit back a sharp retort. 'He did everything by the book. He wasn't psychic. No one was expecting an attack on that scale.'

'Of course not. Do continue.'

Felix looked up at the ceiling, smooth and featureless, a void. 'In the dream, I'm watching my dad trudge over to the target, weighed down with his bomb suit and equipment. It's baking hot . . .' He shook his head, not wanting to go there. Especially not when the other memories were still so fresh in his mind. 'You must have my notes there. You've got to know this stuff.'

'Take your time. I need you to talk me through it.'

Felix pushed out a deep breath and resolved to stay calm. 'It's like I'm right there with him. I watch him shuffle forward the last few metres. I can see the timing and power unit poking out of the holdall. The brains of the bomb. Daring Dad to make a mistake. Willing him to.'

The ceiling was so white, like a perfect drift of snow. Calm. A soothing blankness.

'Felix?'

'Dad sets up the tripod. Manhandles the disruptor over the top of the holdall, ready to take a downward shot into the device – shatter the firing pack. Once the disruptor's in place he walks back down the platform, then down onto the tracks and into the tunnel.' He paused, fighting to control his breathing. 'He pulls off his helmet, gives his number two the nod . . .'

Jenson rifled through some pages of notes. 'The descriptions of your father's actions seem very detailed and accurate for a non-combatant.'

Felix scowled. Shrinks could never be bothered to actually read your whole file. 'Dad kind of took his work home with him,' he explained. 'Mum was never around to stop him sharing it with me. So I lived every job with him. I know what he would've done, and how he'd have gone about it, the procedural stuff. And now I'm well-trained in it myself.'

'Of course.' Jenson didn't look up. 'Go on.'

'Dad fires off the disruptor, takes out the bomb's heart. The timing and power unit's scattered over the platform with bits of explosive, but he needs to find the dets. There are components all over the place. If a battery comes into contact with the detonator's leads he could still be . . . be . . .'

Silence. White. Calm. *Swallow hard.*

'He could be blown to bits,' Felix said matter-of-factly, itching his side, fiddling with the wires. 'So, carefully he twists the ends of the detonator's leads together and eases the det from the block of high explosive. He lays out the components on the dropsheet. Takes his knife and cuts a small piece of explosive away from the main charge. And right there and then he knows it's plasticine. Another hoax. No threat.'

'Because the threat's up above, isn't it?' The shrink's voice had hardened. 'Your dad's just one of scores of experts in IED disposal called out to the Heathrow area on hoax calls.'

Felix nodded, shivered. 'Gathered for the slaughter.'

'I can't imagine you've ever forgotten those images, Felix, the way the media played and replayed them, over and over . . .'

'How can anyone forget?' Felix could feel the electrodes against his skin, his heart thudding out a harder rhythm as, unbidden, his mind seemed to project the hated, sickening CCTV footage onto the blank screen of the ceiling. *A cement truck veers off the A4 and smashes through Heathrow's northern perimeter fence. Screaming across the North Runway towards Terminal Three. An identical cement truck crashes through the fence running alongside the A30. It roars across the South Runway towards the terminal building—*

'When did you first realize your father had to be dead, Felix?'

Felix felt the question like a punch. 'I . . . I kept hoping . . .' He could hardly speak, anger choking the words in his throat. He willed himself to be calm. *It's just a test. You'll get through it.* But he couldn't stop the rush

of images now, coming as they always came in his
recurring dream.

*So many passenger jets on the ground, waiting to taxi
out onto the runway. Each one tanked up with close to
two hundred tonnes of high-octane aviation fuel. The
trucks reach the terminal building within a second of each
other. Screech to a halt either side of a 747. Armed police
race to the scene. Heroes – they're gonna take out the
bad guys . . .*

'How many hours did you have to sweat it out before
you knew for sure that your dad wasn't coming back?'

'The call came that evening.' *Security too slow. The
truck bombs detonate, blow up the 747 between them.
Its fuel tank ignites. Firestorm. Chain reaction.* Felix closed
his eyes, tried to slow his breathing. *Jet after jet explodes
in a screaming cacophony of roiling flame and noise, tearing apart the terminal. Windows shatter, metal buckles.
There are thousands of people caught inside – torn apart,
nuked to nothing as the entire airport's levelled. Even the
planes taking off are blown up, the shockwaves tearing
others from the sky, crippling them as they career into
tower blocks, smash through bridges and houses, crash
through parks and playgrounds, wipe out hundreds and
hundreds more . . .*

Dr Jenson wasn't letting up. 'When your father felt
the shockwaves . . . do you think he guessed that
Orpheus had lured him here to be killed with all the
innocents above?'

Felix bit his lip, scissoring the skin till spots of blood
welled up. *He's pushing you. Wants you to react.* 'The

dream ends when' – he swallowed, tasting iron – 'when the roof falls down on Dad.'

'Just as in real life. There were no survivors, were there? Took days to pull the bodies from the wreckage—'

'That's when I always wake up,' Felix interrupted. He listened to his breathing snag at the silence, felt the sick throb in his temples slowly ebb. 'But now it's almost two years later, and I'm *really* waking up. I've driven myself to get to a position where I can make a difference.' He stared into Jenson's cold, stony eyes. 'I'm guessing I'm here because some ATLAS head shed thinks I've got a personal score to settle, thinks my judgement might be clouded. Well, it isn't – whatever your machine says. I'm not just out for revenge – I want to play my part in making sure something like this never happens again. We need to take Orpheus apart, take it down – from the bomb emplacers and their support teams to the insurgent command and control networks.'

'That's a fine speech.' Jenson stood up, his sweater tightening over hidden muscles. 'But I've seen your kind before, Smith. You think you're special 'cause you made it through to the end of the ATLAS course. You've scraped together a few weeks' tradecraft and suddenly you think you're Jimmy Bond, isn't that right? Think you're ready for big boys' rules.'

Felix yanked off the electrodes and swung his legs off the couch, puzzled and angry. 'What the hell was my intensive training for, if—'

'You come in here talking so big about what an asset

you're going to be to Minos . . . and yet you took this whole scenario at face value.' Dr Jenson pulled a fighting knife from his belt. 'Didn't you?'

Felix stared in disbelief as the world seemed to tilt to one side. 'What the . . . ?'

'You wanted to leave your mark, Smith?' Jenson snarled. 'Well, you will. And that mark's gonna be blood-stains on the carpet . . .'

Desperately Felix threw himself aside as the shrink threw the knife and it stuck into the leather couch. Without even thinking, he hit the ground, performed a shoulder-roll and jumped back to his feet – he'd practised the move so often it had become lodged in his muscle memory. As time seemed to slow, as his momentum carried him forward, he heard Major Fawcett's words cut through the fug in his head: *If there's absolutely no choice but to fight, it has to be hard, fast, unexpected and merciless. Before you land the first blow, you must visualize exactly what you're going to do to your opponent. When you do . . . then you'll unleash hell.*

Jenson yanked a SIG pistol from a hip holster under his jacket, and aimed it between Felix's eyes. But Felix slapped it away with the back of his hand, grabbed his assailant's wrist across the desk, twisted it round over his shoulder and slammed it down against the desk edge. The move wrenched a snarling shout of pain from Jenson – till Felix filled the man's open mouth with his fist. Jenson's head cannoned back against the wall with a loud smack and he slumped to the floor, a dribble of blood leaking from his purple lips.

The door to the office was thrown open behind Felix, and he whirled round to find two huge men bundling inside with assault rifles. He looked for Jenson's gun but it was on the floor out of reach. Whoever these men were, they had him cold. He raised his hands and stood stock-still as they covered him with their M16s . . .

And then the spook from the afternoon's test exercise walked in, his face craggy and cold as sunless cliffs. *I've blown Minos*, Felix realized. *I've so blown it*. He closed his eyes, waiting for the worst, the throb in his bruised knuckles signalling the slow ebb of adrenaline.

The spook ignored the man on the floor and studied the machine that had recorded Felix's stats. 'You really thought we'd use graphs and pulse rates to see if your emotional response to Day Zero would leave your judgement skewed?' He looked over at Felix and smiled. 'In your position, strength of mind is as important as physical ability. After hours of gruelling simulation, we left you racked with uncertainty as to the outcome. We sent you to an area calculated to disorientate you with painful memories. Then our man Jenson – posing as a figure in a profession you've been conditioned to trust your whole life – made you relive your worst nightmare before attacking you without warning.'

Felix reacted as the men facing him lowered their guns and stepped smartly backwards. 'This was all a come-on? Mind games?'

'Training,' the grey man insisted. 'Unorthodox by regular forces standards, I know. But then, you're not with the regular forces any longer.' He smiled tightly.

'Congratulations. You neutralized Jenson's threat swiftly and without injury to yourself. As of now, your training is complete and you're ready for active service – typically in battlespaces where the disabling and removal of improvised explosive devices will play a key role.'

The words made sense slowly. *I did it.* The flood of relief that smashed through Felix was so intense he almost staggered. *I actually did it!* He tried to wipe the shocked expression from his face, to act grown-up and seemly. 'Uh . . . thank you. Sir. Can I ask, did . . . did Pete Adams make it too?'

'I'm afraid you'll be having no further contact with your colleagues from the course, for the time being at least,' the spook said. 'You were the only successful candidate from your wave. You're one of ours now, Mr Smith. Welcome to the Minos Chapter.'

A Mercedes CL-Class was waiting for him outside the building. Felix scrambled into the back. The driver acknowledged him with a nod and then pulled away.

The route out of London seemed tortuous – whether for security reasons or bad traffic, he hadn't a clue. He felt drained, exhausted. But his mind was still fizzing like he'd just downed a vat of Red Bull. Was Jenson a real shrink, or just a spy who borrowed the man's offices when ordered to spring nasty surprises on new recruits? And would Jenson now see a real doctor, or someone posing as a doctor, to analyse his failure to nail Felix?

To nail ME. The only successful candidate. Felix shook his head as a giant grin took hold of his aching cheeks for the fiftieth time. *You did it, you did it, you bloody did it!* Then the grin faded as he thought of Private Pete and wondered how he must be feeling right now. Most likely he was already filling in a further application for attachment to ATLAS. *You'll get in next time, mate*.

As he was driven along the M25, Felix clocked the gleaming signs already pointing to New Heathrow Airport. It was due to open in a little over two weeks, marking the two-year anniversary of Day Zero; a crazy deadline that no one had believed possible to meet. But with most powers in the world contributing skills, design or equipment to the project, it looked set to become a reality. Though it could never again be just an airport, of course. It was two global fingers held up to the scum who thought they could win change through mass murder. And as such, it would remain a target for any maniac with a point to prove. Security would have to be tighter than a camel's butt in a sandstorm. But Felix suspected the passengers wouldn't be complaining about the resulting delays. Not this time.

The car left the London orbital road, heading for the commuter-belt countryside beyond. Felix began to feel uneasy. He'd been tricked and tested twice today already – was this long journey leading to yet another come-on?

He wished he could talk to someone. But who was there left? It seemed obvious that any contact with his regular army mates would be frowned upon. And he had no family left to speak of; after Mum had ditched his dad Felix had made it clear he wanted no part of her new life in Oz. And he hadn't talked to Auntie Mags for almost a year. She'd only agreed to become his legal guardian in the first place for her sister's sake. She'd made out she was angry with him for joining up so young out of fear for his mum – *What will it do to her if you get yourself killed like your father, you selfish little snot?* – but after years playing the single mum without much conviction, it was crystal clear she'd been desperate to be shot of him at the first opportunity. He'd done them both a favour . . .

This is how Minos likes its agents, he reminded himself. *No ties. No distractions.*

Eventually the car pulled up outside a smart hotel hidden at the end of a long winding driveway. Felix tried to catch his driver's eye in the rear-view mirror. 'Uh . . . is this place where I'm going to live?'

'ATLAS personnel are moved around pretty much the whole time,' the driver told him. 'You're no longer a young army recruit. You're whoever your cover story says you are. Sometimes you'll stay in hotels, sometimes you'll be placed with make-believe families, depending on the mission.' He shrugged. 'From now on, Mr Smith, you're of no fixed abode.'

Felix eyed the smart, sculpted sandstone building and raised his eyebrows. 'Well, as somewhere to crash, I guess it's not so bad.' He could hear music blaring out of open French windows. It sounded like there was a party going on.

'I'll check you and your pack in,' the driver announced, and tossed Felix a key. 'You're in room one-eleven. But the night's even younger than you are. You've earned some R and R. So, go celebrate. Make the most of it.'

'Thanks,' Felix told his driver, still wondering if this was all on the level as he got out of the car. He felt completely drained. But the thump and boom of the music was already stirring a little awareness back into his body.

'You heard the man,' he told himself. 'Go celebrate.'

The French windows gave onto a large bar and dining area, studded with leather couches and glass coffee tables. People his age were sitting around, drinking and yelling conversations over the pounding music. Mostly blokes, but some girls too. Crates of drink were stacked on the bar, but Felix could see no staff. Some big rugby-playing types were helping themselves. He decided to go over and grab a bottle of water for starters.

A broad, tall man clocked Felix as he approached. He looked older than everyone else, maybe in his early twenties. His hair was shaved close to his scalp, and his dark eyes matched the colour of his skin. 'New boy?' he demanded.

'Brand new.' Felix took a chilled glass bottle from the bar. 'Is it that obvious?'

'No tag.' The guy tapped a finger against a thin silver chain around his neck, from which a tiny pendant hung. The pendant showed a black trident pointing down so the prongs made an M shape, striking red flame from an open book. Felix saw that the other guys at the bar were wearing them too.

'Minos Chapter,' Felix translated the visual clue.

'I can see you passed your IQ tests.' The big man spoke with an American accent, and his grin was warm. 'We've been waiting for you to show. I'm Zane Samuel.'

'Felix Smith. Good to meet you, sir.' He shook hands and waited to be introduced to the others at the bar. But the guys drifted away into the shadows, leaving him alone with Zane. 'Something I said?'

'Nah. They just can't be bothered to hear me go through the welcome spiel for a third time.' Zane smiled. 'You're the third of three new recruits due tonight. One from New Delhi, one out of Michigan—'

'And the north London boy,' Felix broke in. 'So you're the welcome wagon, sir?'

'Enough with the "sir", Felix. I'm here to help orientate you.' Zane shrugged. 'Think of me as the big brother you never had. And the even bigger pain in the butt.'

Felix smiled and looked around. 'So, is this a Minos HQ?'

'It's been hired out for the night by a cover organization. The staff believe you're a bunch of gifted students in town for an awards presentation.' Zane finished his bottle and cracked open another. 'We don't have regular HQs, Felix. With no central command, there's nowhere for the enemy to target. No heart they can try to cut out.'

'I guess that figures. My dad told me that's how the internet started up – thanks to the US military, right? By running things from several shared servers across the country, no single enemy strike could take you out.'

'Wow. Metaphors.' Zane smiled to himself. 'Well, your papa was right, and Minos uses the same thinking. You're just one of a group of operatives with no real call to know each other. There'll be no more of your regular army camaraderie. No more of your band of brothers.' He smiled and put a friendly hand on Felix's shoulder. 'It can be tough, especially at first. But smile, man – I'm going to be a regular fixture in your life. Your handler. The main point of contact between the Minos agents on my roster and the headsheds.'

Felix looked at the volume of people in the room. 'I suppose there must be a few of you?'

'Whole ATLAS department.'

'How are agents assigned?'

Zane looked at him. 'They said you asked a whole lot of questions. Guess they were right.' He shrugged. 'It's not rocket science. When a handler loses an agent, he's assigned a newbie.'

Felix nodded. 'When you say "lose" . . .'

'Let's not get too morbid on your first night, huh? Lighten up.' Zane gestured around. 'Now and then, those headsheds make it so a bunch of you can be bussed in someplace to cut loose and party hearty.'

'Sounds good.' Felix raised his eyebrows as Zane pulled a Thuraya satphone from his pocket and placed it down on the bar. 'Bet that sounds good too.'

'This is your lifeline. Hotline to Minos manned by the terror-heads.'

Felix took the phone and saw there was a single number programmed into the memory. 'Manned by the who?'

'You'll see. They're kind of freaky, but wherever you are, they're always there too at the end of the line. Data retrieval, operational support, that kind of stuff. And they can put you straight through to me.' Then Zane placed a small leather pouch into his other hand. 'Your own chain's in there. It incorporates GPS tracking technology, so you're never off our radar.'

'Wow. OK. Cool.' Felix held the pouch tightly in his fist. 'So, I'm really in . . .'

'That's the score,' Zane agreed. 'Till you're sixteen, anyway.'

Felix swigged from his bottle. 'Once you're sixteen you're past it?'

''S right. We got a couple of fourteen-year-olds, but mostly fifteen is the magic number. Sweet sixteen and you're out of Minos and into retirement on a full military pension. Or if you're going career with ATLAS, it's onwards and upwards.' He looked at Felix. 'You didn't waste time, did you? Joined up the second the law changed.'

Felix nodded. 'Pretty much.'

'Family in the military, right? That's how it worked for our first few waves of recruits.' Zane swigged the last gulp of his beer. 'A few pulled strings here and some red tape cut there to get you onto the fast-track, right?'

'Not exactly,' Felix retorted. 'My dad was killed in Day Zero. Aiden Smith. I should think you've heard of him.'

'Yes, I have.' Zane nodded. 'I'm sorry for your loss, Felix. By all accounts your old man was a good guy.'

'You don't win the George Medal for being just good,' Felix bridled. 'He was the best.'

'In which case, it was a great *big* helping hand you got.'

Felix put down his drink. 'What are you saying, sir?'

Zane shrugged. 'It wasn't easy for ATLAS to get the

government or GI5 to back Minos, *Mr* Smith. Kids learning trades in the army is one thing, but only 'cause they're kept away from the killing grounds till they're seventeen. If it became public knowledge that we're sending minors into war zones to do adult soldiering, simply to try to catch the enemy off-guard . . .'

'It's not like you're forcing us,' Felix shot back. 'Any advantage over Orpheus could mean who knows how many lives saved.'

'Right. Which is why the Minos headsheds won through and the Chapter was started up three months ago. Of course, it needed good people straight away, gifted naturals who could get results and justify Minos's existence. So, promising young soldiers around the globe with strong military backgrounds were rushed onto the training course and—'

'You think I'm only here because of my dad?' Felix felt a burn of resentment. 'Do you have any idea of what I went through to prove I have a place here?'

'Nope,' Zane said evenly. 'And while you stand there trading on your daddy's rep instead of your own, I guess I never will.'

The words stung Felix like a slap in the face. And the truth of them made them bruise all the more.

'Look around, Felix. This room's full of good kids who lost someone in Day Zero, or in the Canberra bombings, or at Mumbai or wherever. Excellent young soldiers whose desire to get back at Orpheus drove them that little bit harder.' Zane paused. 'Don't get me wrong. Their connections saw them picked out, but it was their ability that got them through.' He cracked open another beer. 'I'm just saying that, living or dead, your family can't do you any more favours. It's you who's got to impress now. You, and everyone else in this room, have a duty to show Minos's critics in GI5 that they were wrong – by making good and getting real results.' He grinned, a genuine, friendly look in his eyes. 'And it's also your duty to large it tonight, big-time. Everything's on the taxpayer – you don't want it going to waste, right?'

Felix smiled grudgingly. 'I guess not.'

'End of pep talk,' Zane declared. 'Now, get out of here. Have fun.'

'But . . . when do I start?' Felix persisted. 'What's my first assignment? What about—'

'I said, go!' Zane waved him away good-humouredly. 'Celebrate! Enjoy!'

Swigging his posh bottle of water, Felix wandered off and sat down at a table alone. He pressed the cold glass against his burning cheeks. *However I got here*, he thought, *I'm going to prove I belong. Whatever it takes.*

He wondered if the people here were looking at him just as he'd looked at the recruits in the firing range this afternoon – remembering how they'd used to be. He supposed that in this game you learned to change and adapt fast, or not at all.

Although tonight, hardly anyone seemed to be dwelling on stuff. They were drinking and chatting in excited huddles, or up and dancing. Some were all over each other, having fun while they could. Felix smiled. What was the point in dwelling on the unknowable when he should be celebrating as instructed? The night had definite possibilities . . .

Just then, a stocky girl with cropped red hair loomed up, smiling and swaying. 'I want to snog someone,' she announced in a high, clipped voice. 'Up for it?'

Felix frowned. 'I'm sorry?'

'Why? You've not done anything, *boet*. Not yet, anyway.'

'Boet?'

'As in "mate". Brother. Homie.' She leaned over and her grin grew wider. 'I'm South African – can't you tell?'

'Oh, right.' He shrugged, smiled. 'I'm Felix.'

'Hannah. So how about that snog?' She had good teeth, wasn't bad looking – and clearly wasn't fussy either. 'Jeez, did you dop basic seduction technique at training?'

'Dop?'

'Fail!' She shook her head, smiled again. 'Hint: saying "I want to snog you" is an IOI – indication of interest.' She paused, the smile dropped. 'Look, I almost died today. Life's short, you can't waste a second.'

'I . . .' Felix had no idea how to answer, swigged quickly from his drink. 'I, uh, just got here.'

'Oh?' Her face darkened. 'You're saving yourself for someone better, hey?'

'No,' Felix protested, 'I didn't mean it like that.'

'Ja. Whatever, boet.' With a look as hard as her skinned knuckles, Hannah lurched away on her mission.

Felix watched her go and felt bad. He'd put her glassy

stare down to drunkenness, but now he suspected a part of it spoke of shock.

'So, *are* you saving yourself for better things?'

Felix turned to his left to find a small, slim girl had sat down beside him. With her black bobbed hair, high cheekbones and large, sunken eyes she looked vaguely Eastern European, an impression enhanced by the trace of accent he'd caught over the music. She was smiling, a little forlornly.

'To be honest, I'm not sure what I'm doing,' Felix confessed.

'Honesty? Wow. An honest spy, huh?'

'Well, I am new to this.' Felix raised his eyebrows. 'How about you – an old hand?'

'I fell into this a whole week ago.' Her eyes seemed distant. 'Long week.'

'Long few months,' Felix rejoined. 'At least, it was feeling that way.'

She looked straight at him, dark eyes glinting. 'Until what?'

He bottled it, cleared his throat, embarrassed. The girl smiled. 'Do you want a drink?' he asked.

'I've had one.'

'I'm Felix—'

'I know. But do you know what they've started to call us? What the other GI5 departments call Minos, I mean.' She leaned forward, her eyes fixing him as he shook his head. 'The Split-second Squad.'

He considered. 'That's actually quite cool.'

'I thought at first they meant our reflexes. Our snap

decisions.' She shook her head. 'They're talking about life expectancy.'

Felix thought of Zane's ever-changing roster of Minos agents to mentor, and shivered. 'Well, then. We'll just have to prove them wrong.'

'I hope so.' The girl's smile became a shade more wicked. 'You know, you shouldn't have upset Hannah.'

'Is she your friend?'

She shook her head. 'Friends aren't a good idea here.' Then she got up abruptly. 'Goodbye, Felix.'

Felix half rose from his seat. 'You're going?'

She shrugged, flicked her hair. 'Like I said. Long week.'

'What's your name, anyway?'

'Need to know, Felix.' The girl tapped the side of her nose, her smile hovering about her lips but never quite getting there. 'I guess I'll be hearing from you.'

'You will? But I—'

'Stay lucky.'

She turned and left, with smooth, measured steps. Felix watched her go. She didn't look or wave at anyone as she left. Just passed from the bar like a phantom.

This is why it's best just to smile at girls as you run past, he told himself.

Felix looked around and noticed Hannah was now hanging from the neck of one of the big rugby-playing types he'd seen earlier. Well, good for her. He yawned; he felt absolutely shattered, but knew he was too wired to sleep.

So instead, Felix got up, approached a group of guys

laughing uproariously across the room and got ready to introduce himself.

Let the party commence!

Felix woke to the piercing trill of an alarm clock. He groped for it blindly on the table beside the bed and shut it off with a groan. He felt as rough as a cat's tongue in a sandpaper sandwich.

Forcing his eyes to focus, he found it was four-thirty a.m. Who'd set his alarm – the driver? Zane? A practical joker? He remembered leaving the party at close to three, staggering into his room and crashing out the moment he touched the soft bed. Looking down, he found he was still fully dressed in his sweat-stinking clothes. It had been a good night, spent mainly with a bunch of Aussies, swapping training nightmares and the filthiest jokes they could think of.

Felix drifted off to sleep again then woke with a start. It was almost ten past five. If that alarm call had been legit, he needed to get seriously motoring. Then he noticed his backpack on the floor. With a twist of alarm, he realized it looked empty. Climbing slowly out of bed, he found his kit had actually been transferred to a large, dirty backpacker-style rucksack. *Guess the Bergen might stand out a bit undercover*, he supposed. A cool, slimline laptop sat in a case on top of the chest of drawers, and fresh clothes had been laid out for him – jeans, boxers and a top. Nothing flash. In fact, they looked already worn.

Suddenly he realized the handle of the door to the

bedroom was starting to turn. Instantly alert, he jumped out of bed – it was just bad luck he got his foot tangled in the sheets and fell forward flat onto his face.

'Oh, it's you,' came the high South African accent. 'This bodes well.'

Felix looked up to find Hannah looking stonily down at him. 'What is this?'

She eyed his crumpled clothes. 'Come on, playtime's over, boet. We're tasked on surveillance ops together, and a car's coming to collect us. So sort yourself out and let's get going – I'll brief you on the way. You've got five minutes . . .'

She stormed out and Felix heard again the girl's voice in his ears: *You don't want to upset Hannah* . . . How'd she know he'd been put with her, anyway?

'Looks like my split-second life span just got even shorter,' Felix muttered ruefully, stumbling into the bathroom, getting in gear for his first day with Minos.

. . . TWENTY-ONE . . .

It was a weird way of starting work, Felix decided. The car had dropped him and Hannah discreetly in a quiet street in Ruislip and they'd got an early tube train into the west London suburb of Northolt. Having woken up a little, Felix had wanted to discuss whatever assignment lay ahead for him, but the noise of the rattling tube made that impossible without being overheard. Hannah kept up the silent act as they got off the train, and Felix wondered if she was still in a mood with him over last night.

The morning had grown warmer and his tiredness had faded. After a breakfast of bacon butties and thick black coffee from a run-down café, the two of them went to hang out in the concrete gardens of a big tower block. Felix sat on a broken bench with his backpack between his legs watching old people shuffle about with shopping, gangs of hoodies shouting and strutting, and young mums whisking their little ones nervously through the underpass. He understood now why he'd been given used clothing. If he was dressed in new gear he'd have stood out a mile.

Felix was impatient for his briefing, but thought perhaps he should make more of an effort to befriend Hannah first, after their not-great start the night before. He put on a deep, cinema voice-over style accent. 'They promised him glamour . . . excitement . . .'

'It's a dump,' Hannah agreed. 'But you can see why Minos want us here. So many kids just hang out all day, playing hookie from school. Who'd notice two more?'

'This is your first assignment?'

'Ja. I've been holed up with my surrogate dad in a two-bedroom flat with hot and cold running cockroaches for two weeks now.'

'Two bedrooms?' Felix frowned. 'And I'm sleeping . . . ?'

'There's a couch.'

'I'll share it with the cockroaches.' Felix nodded. 'Is your "dad" all right, then?'

'Captain Sommers, retired SAS,' said Hannah. 'Minos thinking is that on undercover missions, if we're going to convince the enemy we're just ordinary kids, we need normal families around us. Well, single parents mostly to save on manpower.'

'Is that a real pain?'

Hannah shrugged. 'Sommers is kind of touchy about coming back to work as a babysitter. He thinks his age and experience should make him my superior – but they don't. We're here as a team, and Zane runs us both.'

'Bet he has his hands full with you.'

'Hey.' She half smiled. 'Zane suggested you pose as my cousin, over on a visit. And I bliksem my cousins, so watch out.'

'Bliksem?'

She clicked her raw knuckles. 'Beat them up.'

'I'm watching, I'm watching,' Felix assured her.

Hannah smiled, gazing around. 'Sums up my last two weeks. Nothing but surveillance duties, so far – until last night.'

'You said . . . you almost died?'

'Forget all that,' she said stiffly. 'Anyway, Zane wanted me to brief you on the situation. And what's really bugging the spooks is that over the last few weeks, a number of suspected terrorists with links to Day Zero have shown up in Britain.'

Felix nodded. 'And one of them is right here?'

'Third-floor flat, eleven o'clock,' Hannah told him. 'Lili Vigas.'

'Sounds like a stripper or something.'

'You wish. She's highly educated, with a thing for political extremists. Normally based in Latvia but she's been in the UK for the last month. Hangs out with a very nasty crowd. Including known bomb-makers.'

'So, is that why I'm here?' Felix eyed the flat. 'To check her place in case it's a bomb factory, make it safe?'

'According to Zane, that's not likely – but he's assigned you here in case he's wrong.' Hannah paused while an old man tottered past their bench, and lowered her voice further. 'You know Orpheus always have a couple of skelms videoing their exploits?'

'Course. Gain intelligence on our responses if the bomb doesn't blow, gain propaganda if it does.'

'Well, Lili was one of those videoing Day Zero.' Hannah looked into Felix's eyes. 'Pro camcorder, sixteen-times optical zoom, sitting pretty in a helicopter. Taping my uncle as he died trying to get others out of the flames.'

My dad was killed too, he almost said, *Aiden Smith*. But this time he bit his tongue. Grief wasn't a competition. 'I'm sorry. Did your uncle live over here?'

'He was a firefighter. And in the TA.' She looked down at the filthy pavement. 'Anyway. D'you catch that documentary on Day Zero on the anniversary?'

Felix shook his head. *Think I need reminding what happened?* 'No.'

'The doc makers advertised online for any amateur video footage of the DZ aftermath for possible use. They got tons of tapes. Going through them, it turns out someone caught the helicopter on tape in the background, a few miles away in Shepperton. Security forces were informed. And high-res enlargement of a couple of frames shows that skinny slag Lili's face, clear as crystal. So ATLAS tracked her down, and—'

'Result.' Felix felt a shot of adrenaline kick through him. 'So, when do we go in and get her?'

'It's not that straightforward,' Hannah told him. 'We know Orpheus are planning something big. Chances are, Lili will be asked to shoot the little souvenir movie again, or contribute in some other way. She might have been asked already. So we keep tabs on her, round the clock. I've hidden listening devices behind her plug sockets and the techies have hacked into her computer's web connection. Sommers has set up a wireless webcam outside the front door. It transmits to his laptop so he can record to the hard drive. He's IDing anyone who passes her doorway.'

'Where is he now?'

'In someone else's flat – one that overlooks Lili's,' she said. 'Posing as a plasterer working for the council.'

'But if this is a routine surveillance job and Sommers is about the whole time . . . how come you nearly died last night?'

'That's the laugh – it had nothing to do with Minos.' Hannah shook her head. 'This gang of jackals from a rival estate saw me coming back from the cashpoint in the Seven-Eleven. Tried it on with me. I had to kick seven shades out of them. One breeker couldn't take the humbling. Put a ball-bearing gun to my head, screamed in my face how he was going to kill me . . .'

Felix could see the echoes of the trauma in her eyes. 'What happened?' he said softly.

'I managed to drop him with a forearm smash to the throat. Close one.' She frowned. 'Of course, I couldn't go to the police, can't afford to draw attention. And his buddies had already taken off, so I took his wallet, made it seem like a mugging, and left him lying there. The skelm was minted up too. Must've had a good day . . .'

'Till he tried it on with you,' Felix murmured. 'Hey, speaking of cashpoints, though,' he said, changing the subject and trying to lighten the mood, 'what do we do for money in Minos? How do we get paid, what do we get? No one's said anything, and I didn't like to ask . . .'

'If you stayed through training, they've probably guessed that moolah isn't your prime motivation in life.' She smiled. 'I got a new cash card and PIN a couple of days in. All agents draw on the same Minos account. No cash limits, but if you take the mick, Zane will come down on you like an RPG attack. Meantime, your weekly wage is paid directly into a secure account; you get access when you leave.'

'Weekly, huh,' Felix noted. 'Like they don't expect us to last the month.' *Split-second Squad, just like the Girl said.*

The next moment, a high, desperate shriek from an upper-storey window to his left was flung out into the concrete arena. Felix got to his feet, but Hannah held him by the hood and yanked him back down. 'Cover, you dummy, remember?' She pulled out her satphone. 'We're not cops and there are no knights in armour around here.'

Felix saw she was right – people were just walking by like they hadn't heard a thing. 'It sounded like it came from—'

'Lili's apartment, I know.' Her call was taken. 'Hi, Dad? Did you hear . . . ?' She frowned. 'No visitors? But it sounded like . . .'

The next moment, a tall, black-clad man swung himself over Lili's balcony, agile as a cat. He dropped down onto the lip of the balcony below and stared at Hannah for a few moments, almost defiantly. Then he leaped out of sight.

A second later Felix heard the jagged, tangled sound of breaking glass and jumped up, grabbing his pack. 'Either that's the biggest cockroach on record or your dad's been sleeping on the job.'

Hannah said nothing, already sprinting away across the concourse towards the entrance to the block. Holding his pack by the straps, he caught her up and kept pace beside her. *Here we go, then*. His heart was beating wildly; sensing, perhaps, that this might be its last chance to make some noise.

He and Hannah burst through the double doors to find the man hurtling down the stairs towards them. A balaclava covered his face, with only dark eyes and a thin-lipped mouth on show.

Without hesitation, Hannah threw herself into the man's path. But somehow the man launched into the air like an expert in *parkour* and flipped over her in a neat somersault. Hannah struck the stone steps where he'd been standing with a cry that echoed up the stairwell, while the man dropped to the floor with barely a sound.

Felix found fear giving way to focus as his training took over. *This isn't a training task. Make it count.* He hurled his backpack at the masked man's feet, forcing him to jump over it – and straight into a smack to the stomach. The guy doubled up. *Got him hard*, thought Felix, jubilant for a moment – until his assailant suddenly head-charged him. Felix was knocked sprawling against the wall. He made to bring both fists down on his attacker's back, but the man brought his head up under Felix's chin and followed through with a blow to the windpipe. Felix clawed at his throat, gasping and retching, unable to breathe.

But by now Hannah had recovered, grabbed their attacker from behind in a headlock. The masked man broke her grip by driving both elbows into her ribs, then swung round and punched her in the face. As she staggered back into the banister rail, he aimed a savage kick at her kneecap, flashed a sneering smile at Felix and fled outside.

Felix made to go after him. 'No,' said Hannah as she rose, flushed and clearly in pain. 'I'll follow, I know the area. You get upstairs. Lili . . .'

'The scream,' Felix remembered. As Hannah tore off in pursuit, he picked up his pack and climbed the stairs three at a time, his throat burning with every swallow. But adrenaline kept the rest of the pain at bay and lent sharpness to his thoughts. Questions and possible answers chased through his head faster than his heart smacked against his ribs.

How did the man reach Lili without Sommers seeing? He must have known Sommers was watching from his vantage point in the council flat and chosen his moment. *But how did he know?*

Felix hoped Hannah wasn't hurt so badly she wouldn't catch up with the masked man. Another assault, so soon after last night's – what were the chances? Well, maybe around here, pretty high, but . . .

He suddenly thought of the way their attacker had hesitated on the balcony. He'd stared at Hannah, ignoring Felix completely. Almost like he was daring her to come after him. Did the masked man know that Hannah had been keeping Lili under obs? If he'd seen her fighting the gang last night, he'd know she was highly trained in close-quarters combat. *Military* trained . . .

And Felix stopped running, his mind firing wildly, snatching at connections. He remembered Hannah remarking on the stack of cash in the gang leader's wallet. *What if the lads had been paid for attacking her?* If Lili or someone had clocked Hannah hanging around and grown suspicious, what better way to get her to break cover and demonstrate her training . . .

No, that was crazy. He was getting paranoid.

Pressing on, Felix soon reached the door to Lili's flat. It was closed, and he was about to try to kick it down. But then he froze.

Lili had screamed out just now to get attention, and the man in black had exited via the balcony, where he could be seen by just about anyone. Why not exit discreetly through the front door?

Unless he didn't because he couldn't. Felix remembered the sneering smile and a sudden realization slammed whatever breath was left in his lungs as he backed away. 'He rigged it,' Felix breathed. He could almost smell the cordite, sense the tension in the tripwire the other side of the door. 'Son of a bitch, this whole thing was a trap.'

. . . TWENTY . . .

Felix could hear a woman's muffled whines coming from inside the flat, high and frantic in tone. Lili. A recording, perhaps? Part of a scam meant to get Hannah or Sommers charging into the apartment and so blow themselves and the tower block to bits?

'I'm here to help,' he called recalling stock phrases from his hostage-rescue training. 'Please indicate that you can hear me.'

The muffled groans swelled in alarm. Lili was in there all right. Gagged, by the sound of things. And she didn't sound happy about someone racing to her rescue.

Pounding feet on the concrete landing behind him made Felix turn. A short, broad man in dull overalls was rushing towards him.

'Mr Smith?' The man put sarcastic emphasis on the

'mister'. 'I'm Mike Sommers, working with Hannah. I've called ATLAS for back-up to catch that clown who got past you.'

'He got past your cameras first,' Felix said defensively.

'Fair play.' Sommers seemed to take the point. There was a Scottish rasp to his accent, as dour as the expression on his florid face. 'What do you think we've got in there?'

'Trouble,' Felix replied. 'I think that "clown" must have tumbled that you and Hannah were keeping obs on this place. Lili's inside there, gagged and most likely bound as well – either she's done something to upset Orpheus or else they're just not prepared to work with someone they think's compromised. So our mystery man has rigged an IED in her flat and then invited us in to have a blast. I don't know yet whether it's on a timer or set to be tripped in some way when the door opens—'

'We need to find out.' Sommers swore, kicked the wall opposite. 'Like I say, back-up is coming.'

'Back-up?' Felix frowned and opened his pack to reveal the tools and instruments inside. 'Zane put me on this assignment. He must have figured I could handle it.'

'He figured you would be able to identify and catalogue equipment in a possible bomb factory,' Sommers retorted, 'not play superhero. You're fresh out of training.'

'And we could be fresh out of time, any minute now,' Felix said, trying to stay cool and not wind up the old soldier further. 'I'd welcome some help, of course I would. But if we wait and whatever's behind that door goes off in the meantime . . .'

'God help us,' Sommers muttered. 'I'd better evacuate the whole area.'

'And when back-up does arrive, make sure they check over your flat – if this guy was onto Hannah . . .'

He nodded slowly. 'Yeah, that holds water. All right. I'll get started while you make an assessment.' He left in moody silence, and Felix turned back to the door, inspecting it for any signs of tampering.

There were none.

He reached into his tool bag and rummaged for his small telescopic mirror. *I should've packed this myself*, he thought. *Should've brought my bomb suit too. Yeah, that wouldn't have stood out at all.* He carefully inserted the mirror through the letterbox and turned it 180 degrees clockwise, searching for any signs of an IED.

Nothing.

He repeated the process in the opposite direction – and then he saw it. A small micro-switch, set back slightly from the door and linked to a timing and power unit by a series of interconnecting blue and orange wires. A chill shot through Felix; beneath the TPU he could see a two-kilo block of Tetryl plastic explosive. It was enough to destroy every flat on the floor. Fortunately, as long as the door wasn't opened, he could leave the bomb in situ . . . for now.

This isn't a training exercise. The realization sat heavily on his shoulders. *This is for real. Total failure or complete success – there's no halfway.*

Get this one wrong and you're dead.

As Felix continued manoeuvring the mirror, beads of

sweat started to crawl across the back of his neck. Then he noticed a laser on one side of the hallway pointing towards a small receiver unit on the other. It was a secondary.

Whoever this bomb-maker is, thought Felix, *he's a pro*.

Felix removed the water aerosol spray from his bag and squirted it through the letterbox and into the hallway. The laser beam immediately illuminated. Just as he'd anticipated – a break-beam booby trap.

'Time to get amongst it,' he muttered, and reached into the tool bag again, this time removing the battery-powered rotary cutting tool. He quickly got to work, wrists aching as he cut a laptop-sized panel out of the front door.

With the panel removed, it was time to inch his body through the cavity. *Here we go, then*, he thought. *So this is how it feels to be the lion-tamer sticking his head into the lion's mouth*. Tentatively, arms thrust forward over his head, he wriggled and worked his way inside the entrance hall until he was lying face-to-face with the first of the two bombs. He had to remove the detonator from the device, but before he could, he needed to identify all the components in the bomb. If there was a hidden collapsing circuit, cutting out the detonator would cause it to explode for sure.

Sweating harder now, Felix traced the wires from the micro-switch down into the TPU, and obsessively followed the bundle of cables contained within it. Amongst the bird's-nest of wires he saw a safe-to-arm switch, a nine-volt battery and a couple of LEDs on a printed circuit board. Pretty textbook, nothing unusual there. Next, he traced the wires coming out from the box leading to the Tetryl explosive. This time he saw two detonators wired in parallel. *Good*, he thought, *it's a standard circuit* – exactly what he'd been hoping to see.

He rummaged in the tool bag for a pair of snips, memories of his intensive training mingling with lessons from his father, stretching back years. The twin-flex wire attached to the detonator had to be cut precisely. If the bare copper strands touched each other and completed the circuit, it would be game over. He had to sever one first, then move a couple of centimetres further down the circuit and deal with the second. That way, there was no possibility of the two arching together.

He took a breath, held it for a few seconds, breathed out, and made the first cut. Nothing. Good.

The spook's words of yesterday echoed through his head: *We have high hopes for you, Smith.*

Heart racing, he moved the snips a few centimetres to the right and repeated the process. Still nothing. He did the same to the second detonator and pulled both free from the explosive.

Felix closed his eyes and let go of a breath he hadn't known he was holding. One down, one to go.

With the first IED neutralized, Felix edged his way forward to the laser device. Once again he studied the bomb, following its circuitry again and again, like re-reading the same sentence in a book until it made sense.

You've scraped together a few weeks' tradecraft and

suddenly you think you're Jimmy Bond, Jenson had snarled, *isn't that right?*

He couldn't see the entire circuit, and he couldn't risk using his disruptor in this scenario – disruptors were good, but there was still a chance the bomb could detonate when using them. He knew that somehow he was going to have to breach it.

Felix studied the circuit once more, and an idea came to him. The laser emanating from the transmitter was pointing across the hallway to a receiver containing an LDR – a light-dependent resistor. He remembered his dad talking about them; as long as the LDR was receiving a laser beam – any laser beam – the bomb would remain in stand-by mode. Felix decided to try and trick the receiver unit by using the battery-powered laser unit in the kitbag. 'Watch it and weep,' he muttered, moving it carefully and precisely right up to the aperture of the receiver. 'One point two milliwatts of hell.'

With the original laser now bypassed and rendered useless, Felix had freedom of movement along the hallway. He stuck two fingers up at the compromised receiver and cautiously started to explore the rest of the flat.

He soon found Lili in her poky, damp-smelling bedroom – gagged, tied up on her bed and strapped into a bomb harness. She looked to be in her late twenties, with long black hair and honey-brown skin. Her ankles were bound and her arms tied behind her back. A huge slab of sticking plaster glued her lips together, but as she stared at Felix her eyes conveyed her fear and helplessness more eloquently than words ever could.

'It's all right,' he said soothingly. 'I'm here to help you.' That's what they told you to say in training – the bomber's victim might be the scum of the earth but you had to go in like you were best mates so they wouldn't struggle and blow you both sky-high. Lili, however, still looked terrified. 'It's OK, uh . . . I'm older than I look. Really.'

As Lili tried to settle herself, trembling and breathing in spiky gasps, Felix studied the device – a fishing vest with blocks of Tetryl explosive sewn into it, linked to an electro-mechanical timer and a mobile phone – presumably for the bomber to use as a back-up means of radio-controlled detonation should the timer fail.

Fighting back a rising panic, Felix inspected the timer. It had stuck fast. When had it been supposed to trigger the blast? How long before the bomber set it off remotely, before the ring tone would sound its electronic death knell . . .

He scrabbled through his kitbag, hunting for an ECM jammer – or a 'modular wireless communications jammer' as his tutors would have had it, capable of blocking out remote control frequencies such as mobile phone signals. There it was. He yanked it out and reverently held it like King Arthur must've cradled the Holy Grail. Only once he'd switched it on and felt the buzz of its transmission begin did he dare relax for a moment and slump down on the bed. If their man in black was trying to detonate the bomb harness remotely, he'd be plugging away a long time.

As if sensing the danger had receded, Lili started to rock impatiently on the bed. 'Don't,' Felix warned her. 'I don't know how stable this setup is. Moving a muscle right now is definitely a bad idea.' He began cutting the fishing vest away from Lili's scrawny body, gently and carefully. Even the slightest jolt could cause the timer to free itself – and there was enough explosive packed around her torso to take out the entire floor of the tower block.

Finally Felix snipped through the last piece of binding fabric and placed the explosives delicately on the floor. 'How was your first day in the new job, Felix?' he murmured, tongue-in-cheek, pushing his sweat-soaked hair back from his forehead. 'It was horrible, thanks.' He looked over at Lili, lying curled up tight on her side as if still waiting for the impact. 'Nice company you keep,' he said coldly. 'I guess you're happier watching this kind of stuff through your camcorder's viewfinder, standing at a distance, right?'

But suddenly Lili lashed out with her legs and knocked Felix sprawling onto the floor. In the moment it took him to fall, he realized that she hadn't just been rocking in a panic – she'd been working her ankles free of the ropes. Now she shifted her weight onto her shoulders, and pulled her bound wrists up and over her hips and legs, so her hands were no longer behind her back. He scrambled up but she grabbed a knife from the bedside table and pounced on him, ready to drive the blade down into his neck.

Then a hefty thump rang out and Lili's eyes glazed over. She pitched forward, landing just beside the vest – to reveal Hannah standing behind her, sweaty and shaking her knuckles.

'Thought I'd check on how you were doing, boet,' she said.

'Thanks.' Felix got unsteadily back to his feet. 'But while I'm defusing a stack of improvised explosive devices? Maybe not the wisest of moves.'

'You weren't looking so clever yourself, just then.'

'Mmm. Why couldn't you have come in when I'd just heroically defused the secondary?' Felix glanced down at the explosives in the vest and the fallen Lili. 'No, on second thoughts, that was good timing.'

'Never mind me. You're in for some real kudos after this.' Hannah looked at him with what might have been respect. 'First day in the job, you pull off a stunt that puts Minos in the best possible light. What's next – going to save the world single-handed?'

Felix looked away, embarrassed. 'Maybe I should thank the guy in the mask for setting the bomb. Did you get him?'

'I didn't,' Hannah admitted. 'But a Ford Focus did. It was changing lanes as he tried to free-run across the fly-over, smacked straight into him. He surfed the tarmac on his head. Not pretty.' She paused. 'No way to go, hey?'

'I guess not.'

'I mean, a Ford Focus? A second later and he'd have been hit by a Merc.'

Felix let out a nervous laugh. 'Any intel on him?'

'He'll be given a good going over. With something more delicate than tyres this time, I suppose.' She paused. 'Sommers says you think he was onto me?'

Felix slumped down on the bed again. 'It was the way

he looked at you from the balcony. I mean, it could have been down to your delicate beauty . . .'

'Ha. Don't forget, what I did to Lili I can do to you.'

'Our masked man must have had an accomplice,' Felix mused; 'someone to signal when Sommers was taking a leak or whatever so he could slip inside.'

'I'm not so sure that's how they did it.' Hannah nodded to Lili's front door. 'Sommers looked through the footage on his laptop out in the car park – according to that, no one called and that door never opened.'

Felix frowned. 'What?'

'There's the *sound* of a door opening. Shortly after, our bug stopped transmitting.' She smiled knowingly when Felix looked blank. 'Want to test a theory and share a little of that kudos you got coming?'

With Lili still unconscious and tied up properly this time, Felix followed Hannah out into the corridor and upstairs in a cloud of wonder and euphoria, replaying events in the flat over and over. *I did it. I beat a bomber. This time.*

Hannah clearly didn't find whatever she was searching for on the floor above, nor the one above that, and from the look on her face she was growing impatient.

'What are you after?' Felix asked.

'Hold on . . .' She led the way back downstairs, this time to the second floor. 'That flat our bomber escaped through, the one below Lili's place . . .' As they arrived outside, she gave a grunt of satisfaction. 'There you go. I'm not just a delicately beautiful face.'

Felix could see nothing out of place. 'What am I

looking at?' The door was still ajar from where the
bomber must've fled through from the balcony to reach
the stairwell where they'd clashed, but . . .

'These doors and walkways all look pretty alike, don't
they?' Hannah wasn't looking at the front door, but at
something small and grey on the wall opposite.
'Surveillance camera,' she explained, 'set at the exact
same angle as the one we trained on Lili's front door. And
our masked man's even changed the door number so this
one says thirty-seven, just like Lili's. It looks identical.'

'That's well devious.' Felix winced as the penny
dropped. 'So our guy swamped transmissions from our
cam with his own signal . . . and jammed the bug when
they got inside.' He looked at Hannah. 'Assuming this is
Orpheus, if they're ready to neg their own operative just
for being under surveillance, and can rig fun and games
like this hours after clocking you as probable military—'

'Then something bloody massive is going down,'
Hannah concluded.

Felix nodded, thinking of the dismantled IEDs upstairs
with a bone-cold chill. 'And something bloody massive
could be going *off*.'

...NINETEEN...

Unlimited funds available from any cashpoint on a daily basis, and Felix had spent all of twelve quid on a bottle of Coke and a large pizza with chicken wings to be eaten back in his hotel room. With the Lili obs blown and a bomber leaving traps for them, the plan to camp out in the crappy flat in Northolt was off.

What a shame, thought Felix wryly. *I should've splashed out on a PS3 or something. Something to help me kick back after DEFUSING MY FIRST REAL IMPROVISED EXPLOSIVE DEVICE.*

The buzz was overwhelming, and the events of the afternoon felt slightly unreal. The sheer scale of all that had gone on – and what could have happened if he hadn't done his job . . . Felix could hardly take it in.

Maybe that was why he was sitting on the bed now, a pepperoni slice in one hand, the other tapping at the keyboard of his Minos laptop. There was no time to celebrate. He might have won a battle but there was still a war to fight.

So now Felix was on a secure link to the archives of TEDAC – the Technical Explosive Device Exploitation Centre, an IED intelligence group based in the US. The components from the bomb in Lili's flat should offer up some quality forensics but in the meantime he'd decided to check for other bombings with a similar style, just in case he could spot a link. It was taking ages.

Felix leaned back and closed his eyes, chewing on a chunk of stuffed crust. Being in Minos, he supposed, was more like being a private contractor than a military bod. There was no return to camp for debriefing or letting off steam with the lads. He and Sommers and Hannah had been whisked away from the scene of the incident in a Minos car and taken back to the hotel. There was no sign now of any of their fellow agents – the 'gifted students' – who'd filled the bar the night before. One of the receptionists, making small talk, had taken Sommers to be Felix and Hannah's father and said how proud of them he must be. He muttered a half-hearted response and went off to the bar to have a drink by himself.

Hannah had eyed Felix as they took the lift back to their rooms. 'Fancy a laugh out somewhere tonight, bru? Think we've earned it.'

'Uh . . . no, thanks. I was thinking of looking through the files for similar IED setups.'

'Ach, get you.' Hannah shook her head. The lift doors opened and she walked out, limping slightly. 'You can save lives and still have one of your own, hey?'

Nice theory, Felix mused. In that moment, as the lift doors had closed, he'd both envied and admired Hannah's ability to switch off. He'd worked and slaved so hard for the chance to join Minos. He'd always told himself that he could do without friends and family to make it on his own, that the sacrifice would be worth it. But now that he *had* made it . . . What next?

There was a knock at the door. Felix was instantly alert, jumping off the bed and crossing the room. 'Who's there?'

'Zane.'

Felix opened the door a crack, eyeballed the big man in the dark, crumpled suit and let him inside. 'Interesting first day, huh?'

Felix shrugged. 'You could say so.'

'More interesting than you know.' Zane sat down heavily on the bed. 'Our teams have been running checks. Seems our piece of terrorist roadkill went by the name of Fenar Rashed; known links to Orpheus, usually based in Turkey. No one had a clue he was in the UK.'

'That's not encouraging,' Felix murmured.

'It's not, is it? We're tracing his movements over the last few days through CCTV footage and anecdotals as we speak . . .' Zane trailed off, noticing the pizza. 'You mind if I . . . ?' Without waiting for permission, he took a bite. 'That's not the interesting bit, by the way. We found Lili's cell phone in Rashed's pocket, pretty much in one piece. And something else.' He pulled out a piece of squared paper and offered it to Felix. 'Seems he took it from Lili's flat. Once he'd got her phone and tied her up on top of that bomb.'

'Removing the evidence . . .' Felix took the paper. It showed a line drawing of six tall, narrow blocks, stretching up vertically and diagonally from a horizontal ink stripe at the base. A further horizontal line had been scrawled just above, as if sectioning off the paper – but the space was empty save for a single cross. 'If he was so sure the place would blow, why not leave this thing behind to go up in smoke?'

'Perhaps he was going to show it to another lensman,' Zane suggested. 'One who wasn't under obs by ATLAS.'

'The vertical patterns look sort of like a skyline,' Felix observed. 'Tower blocks. Targets.'

'And the cross could mark the overwatch position from which Lili – or whoever – was going to film,' Zane agreed through a mouthful of pizza. 'But the diagonal ones . . . who knows? Roads, maybe? Buildings, viewed through some sort of specialist lens?' He shrugged. 'We've gone third degree on Lili to learn more about it. She says it was sent to her by one Supyan Kanska, a terrorist overlord who's wanted in connection with several bombings in the Russian republics.'

'Could she be pulling names out of a hat?'

'I checked in with GI5. They've heard a whisper he's been putting out feelers for good lensmen.' Zane half smiled through another greasy mouthful. 'And here's the clincher. Kanska's signature IED is a dead ringer for the one you dealt with yesterday. Looks likely that Rashed trained under him.'

'It's a link,' Felix agreed. 'So, you think Orpheus has recruited this Kanska guy?'

'In exchange for funding, or training, maybe,' Zane agreed. 'He's meant to be a big-brain and can't have come cheap. Whatever's going down must be big enough to warrant one hell of a spend.'

'Just a bit.' Felix felt the seductive buzz of adrenaline flick through his veins. 'So how do we find Kanska?'

'Lili says the diagram is only part of an overall picture used to co-ordinate the activities of several video crews.' Zane helped himself to another slice. 'Apparently the prospective members of those video crews have been summoned for a briefing in Riga tomorrow night.'

'Where?'

'It's the capital of Latvia. We found an air ticket in Lili's flat, which backs up her story.'

'I mean, where in Riga was she meeting him?'

'She doesn't know. She was waiting for a text that would've given her the precise location.'

'Well, he's not likely to send her one now, is he? Presumably it's Kanska who sent his man Rashed to neg her.' Felix frowned. 'She must have done something to upset him . . .'

'Most likely Orpheus found out she was under obs. They weren't to know that was down to her involvement in Day Zero, not whatever job they've got coming up.' Zane wiped greasy cheese from his lips. 'Even so, the game's not over yet. Lili used to live in Riga. She knows people who know people. She's confident she can track down Kanska.'

Felix pictured her face as she'd tried to bring the knife down on his neck, and shuddered. 'Can we believe her?'

'Her phone's full of contacts, some very tasty names among them. They were all encoded, but as a gesture of good faith she told us how to crack the cipher. Of course, our techies had already worked that out for themselves . . .' Zane smiled. 'By trying to kill her, Orpheus have kind of dented her loyalty to the cause. Now it's just possible that she could lead us straight to someone of high standing in their terror network.' He shook his head. 'There's still a lot we don't understand about their command structure. Alliances between the different terrorist groups seem to wax and wane, but somewhere there has to be a stable committee holding things together, co-ordinating strategy . . .'

Some strategy, thought Felix. *Bomb this place. Bomb that place*. 'What if Lili's feeding you bull because she's looking for a chance to run?'

'It's a possibility,' Zane agreed. 'So you're going with her and Hannah and Sommers to make sure she doesn't take that chance.'

'Oh?' Felix was surprised. 'Why me?'

'Lili's requested it. Now her life's on the line, she wants only agents she's familiar with – reckons others could have been got at.'

Felix felt a twinge of irritation. 'She gets to set terms?'

Zane shrugged his shoulders. 'No point in winding her up when we want her on side. And knowing the company she keeps, having an IED disposal specialist along may be a good thing.'

'Right.' Felix nodded.

'It's gonna be dangerous, but you knew that, right? Orpheus will know Lili's still alive, they'll have seen from the news that the bomb didn't go off. So, we'll lay on a big military flight to an Allied air base in Bulgaria, let it "slip out" that we're holding Lili there. Hopefully, Orpheus eyes will be drawn to that – while you and the others take a commercial flight to Riga tomorrow. Just mum, dad and the kids enjoying a little city break.' He grinned. 'Meanwhile, your kit and weapons will be sent on separately in a Learjet. You did good today, Felix. Put a lot of headsheds in a sunny mood. Think of this little jaunt as a reward.'

Felix smiled wryly. 'It's gonna be one dysfunctional family holiday. Where do we fly from?'

'That'll be decided last minute for security reasons. You'll get a call in the small hours. Make sure you're good to go.' Zane stood up and pushed the last of the pizza into his mouth. 'Wanna know one other thing that was interesting about our masked bomber-man? He was a dead man running even before that car hit him.' He paused, a disquieted look on his rounded features. 'Rashed's body was riddled with tumours that would most likely have killed him within a year. He was suffering from ARS – Acute Radiation Syndrome.'

Felix frowned. 'Radiation poisoning?'

'We're trying to find out what kind of exposure he had, and how long ago.' Zane smiled suddenly, as though shrugging off the black mood, and nodded to the laptop. 'Meantime, quit with the homework, Felix. We have people checking the forensics. You could use some sleep.'

'Understood.' Felix yawned. 'Thanks for helping out by eating my dinner for me.'

'You're welcome.' Zane crossed to the door. 'Next time though, pick one with extra chillies on, OK?'

As the door swung shut, Felix looked down at the messy debris in the pizza box. *I'm off to Latvia with a terrorist, a toughnut South African and an ex-SAS officer. I think things are going to be hot enough as they are.*

The promised call came around three a.m., the shrill tone of his satphone slicing through the night silence. Felix's eyes snapped open as he rolled over to snatch up the receiver.

'Two cars will be coming for you and Hannah in twenty minutes,' came a female voice. 'One will transport your equipment to an air freight company in Woking. The other will be carrying forged passports and air tickets; it will take you and Hannah to Gatwick Airport, where you'll rendezvous with Sommers and Lili Vigas. You'll catch a Czech Airways flight which is due to depart at seven-hundred hours for Riga International Airport.'

'It's you, isn't it?' Felix realized. 'The girl I met at the party.'

A pause. 'Yes.'

'Seems just a split second ago,' Felix went on. 'Is this what you do at Minos – co-ordinate operations?'

'Sometimes.'

'So, what *is* your name?'

'I told you. Need to know.'

Felix wasn't about to grovel for the info. 'Why do they call you people "terrorheads", anyway? Is that as in "war on terror" or is your mind just a scary place?'

'The latter, completely,' said the Girl. 'But it's actually "tera-head" – as in terabyte, which is a thousand times more than a gigabyte, which is a thousand times more than—'

'– a megabyte, yeah, I get it,' said Felix, embarrassed by his blunder. 'Why'd they call you *tera*-heads then?'

'We specialize in high-speed, high-volume data retrieval. Data of just about any kind.'

'You retrieve data but you can't even tell me your name?'

'You wouldn't give your computer a name, would you?' she said, and Felix thought he caught an air of sadness in the reply. 'We're just a resource, Felix. Minos isn't about personal attachments, remember? The fewer the better. Keep things clean.' She paused. 'And be ready in twenty.'

She rang off.

...EIGHTEEN...

Felix sat in the departure lounge with his temporary family, staring at his passport. His picture stared back at him, but his name had become Felix Sommers. His adopted sister Hannah sat beside him, while Sommers himself and Lili were in the seats opposite. They were holding hands – or rather, the burly ex-soldier was holding hers. She didn't seem exactly delighted by the attention, but at least she wasn't creating either. The fear and fury he'd seen in her dark eyes the night before had died; now they showed only resignation.

At least it wasn't too busy. Hannah passed Felix a can of Coke, and he took a swig. The bubbles and the early start made his stomach protest a little; or was that just nerves? He hated airports. The shadow of Day Zero fell a lot more thickly here. Armed guards still made their walkabouts, and armoured vehicles still crawled around the airstrips' perimeters. But Felix still felt horribly vulnerable.

'Wish I had my pack,' he grumbled.

Hannah took back the can and yawned. 'I bet you tuck your rucksack up in bed every night, hey? I bet you cuddle up to your little wire-cutters.'

'A lad of fifteen fiddling with his tool in bed at night?' Sommers grinned. 'Never.'

Felix smiled back at him. 'At least I can find mine.'

'Now, now, boys,' said Hannah quietly. 'Not in front of Mummy. She looks like she's having a bad day.'

'I just want to get on with this,' Lili said in a heavy East European accent. 'I've given so much for those sons of bitches . . .'

'Not as much as they've taken from us,' Felix muttered.

'What happens when we get to Riga?' Hannah asked.

'Lili's going to give us chapter and verse on all the lowlifes and scumbags she knows,' said Somers, 'so we can press them for info on where Kanska's holding his secret briefing.'

Lili muttered something incomprehensible in her own language.

'Mum just said she'll be interested to see how far we get trying to talk English to these people,' Hannah announced. Lili looked suddenly discomfited.

Sommers just smiled, while Felix looked at Hannah with new respect. 'You speak Latvian?'

'*Ar vienu valodu nekad nepietiek.*'

'Huh?'

'One language is never enough.' She shrugged, but

seemed pleased he was impressed. 'You don't think I got into Minos with just my fists?'

'So we'll be fine,' Sommers said, stretching out in his seat. 'Hannah's fluent in Russian too – Latvia's other language. And if Mother here tries to warn them or says one word out of line, we'll know and act accordingly.' He squeezed Lili's hand. 'But since Orpheus has marked her for death, she should know there's nowhere to run. She needs our protection. And she'd better remember that.'

Lili looked down at the floor, her eyes wide and dark. 'How can I forget?'

Felix had only flown a couple of times in his life, back when he was a kid. It was cramped and crowded but that didn't make it any less exciting. He loved the feeling of acceleration as the aircraft tore up the airstrip for takeoff, grateful to be leaving the terminal intact behind him.

He sat with Hannah, while Sommers and Lili took the seats in front of them. The engine's noisy drone filled the space as if holding them in the air through sheer determination. Hannah didn't spare a glance for the view, her eyes fixed on Lili's back, watching for any signs of furtive movement. Sommers read the paper, and only Felix was looking through the window as the North Sea gave way to German forest and then blurred again into the Baltic. His stomach was churning with the knowledge he'd embarked on his first undercover mission. *It's what you've spent so long training for*, he reminded himself. Then he remembered Private Pete joking once that the Minos training course felt like one long suicide note that you signed when you began active service.

It didn't seem so funny any more.

The morning had grown cloudy and cool as they came in to land at Riga Airport, a small modern-looking structure of glass and steel. The runways were full of pot-holes and craters and Felix spied a kind of graveyard for old, rusting planes at one end of the airfield; as they descended, he hoped theirs wouldn't be joining the pile.

As it turned out, the landing was smooth and they were soon taxiing across the tarmac to the terminal build-ing. Sommers took hold of one of Lili's hands again, and Hannah gripped the other tightly like a fond daughter, playing up to their cover.

'We must be nutters, coming here for a holiday,' Sommers joked as they queued at passport control. 'Latvia was part of Communist Russia till 1990. It's one of the poorest countries in Europe.'

'It won the Eurovision Song Contest once,' said Hannah, though Felix wasn't sure if this was meant in Latvia's defence or as another nail in the coffin.

They got through customs without incident, the forged passports passing muster. The arrivals hall was littered with people waiting with bunches of flowers.

'What's all that about?' Hannah wondered.

'You don't know?' Lili smiled waspishly. 'I suppose you only learn other languages so you can make sure your demands are understood. You don't bother yourself with the customs or culture of the country.'

'Izzit?' Hannah shrugged. 'Don't tell me, then.'

'It's a Latvian tradition,' Lili went on regardless. 'There should always be an odd number of flowers in the bouquet. An even number is only for funerals.'

Felix found himself reluctant to look at the blooms too closely as they took the ground-floor exit. *Since when am I superstitious?* he thought, climbing after the others into one of an endless line of red taxis. Hannah instructed the driver to take them to the hotel booked for them in the old town. Felix watched the character of the capital slowly change from big, blocky hotels and industrial buildings to more residential streets. Ornate structures and quaint churches stood out among the down-at-heel wooden housing and soot-stained apartment blocks.

'Where did you live when you were here?' Felix asked Lili.

'Over in the Kengarags district,' she said languidly. 'With a friend.'

'In one of the commie blocks, was it?' Sommers broke in. 'All that grey concrete, lovely. Well, if Orpheus catch up with you now, you'll end up swimming with a chunk of it tied round your neck. Should make you feel at home.'

Lili didn't answer the taunting comments, staring sad-eyed through the window. Felix felt uncomfortable. He supposed Sommers was still smarting from being caught off-guard and was taking it out on her. Felix hated the woman as much as anyone; she had stood filming Day Zero with a smile on her face, glad it had happened. But still, they needed her on side. How was antagonizing her going to help?

Even so, he could imagine the results if he said any-thing. *Been an active agent for five minutes and know it all already, is that it?*

Felix stayed quiet.

The day passed slowly. The boutique hotel was all smart browns and linen luxury, but Felix was too tense to enjoy it. He felt a little happier when an anonymous courier delivered his pack and he could sort through his gear, checking all was present and correct from his snips and ceramic knife to the Goldman portable X-ray generator.

But while Hannah made cautious contact with various of Lili's extremist friends on speakerphone, Felix just felt like a spare part. He worked out in the hotel gym, but the tension was still there twisting through his body so he decided to go for a run. Two mornings on the trot he'd had to sacrifice his usual six-mile warm-up; he had some catching up to do.

Pack on his back, he jogged through the quaint, cobbled streets of the Old Town. It was a bright August day, but cool with it. He took in the sights. Well-dressed women in high heels negotiating the cobbles with easy grace. Old men drinking espressos at pavement cafés, wrapped up against the unseasonal chill in the air. Tourists with cameras, and gangs of guys weaving from bar to bar on all-day stags.

After his run, and a shower, Felix kept a watchful eye around the hotel, scouring the corridors for suspicious activity, looking out at the streets below through each of the grand hotel's picture windows and hanging around in reception.

He jumped as his satphone rang. It was Hannah. 'Felix, where are you?'

'By the front desk,' he told her. 'Just keeping an eye.'

'Well, stay there and I'll be down in a minute.' She sounded excited. 'It looks like we've got the location for Kanska's briefing – a café-bar in some garden suburb.'

'A café-bar?' Felix echoed. 'Doesn't sound the kind of place for a big terrorist get-together.'

'Which is probably exactly why he's chosen it,' Hannah remarked. 'Never heard of hiding in plain sight?'

'I suppose, but—'

'Two of Lili's contacts confirmed independently that he uses the place a lot for discreet meetings, it's practically his office.' Hannah sighed impatiently. 'Look, I'm coming down, hey? Sommers says there'll be no action till eight tonight, so let's go eat. Sightsee. Whatever.'

'Don't you think we should maybe stay with Lili and—'

'Felix, for God's sake! Come on, we're in a foreign country on a big fat expense account. Let's live a little.'

The phone went dead. Felix tucked it away and sat down to wait for her, wondering if food or playing tourist might calm his churning stomach. Wondering if anything could.

... SEVENTEEN ...

Time crawled until it was time to go, even the hours spent chatting over drinks with Hannah in a succession of Old Town cafés. The shadow of the night's mission fell over him, cold and heavy, clouding his attempts at conversation.

Now, at a little after seven, Felix followed Sommers, Hannah and Lili into another red taxi, booked to take them to the Tornakalns district on the other side of the river. He and the others sat in the car just as they had before, except now the tension in the air was strung out between them like tripwires. His SIG 229 handgun nestled in its shoulder holster, chafing his ribs.

I'm armed. It was a strange feeling for Felix, knowing he was carrying a loaded weapon and that he might have to use it. The first year of army training, recruits were issued with plastic bullets – one of the concessions made by the military headsheds to the liberals to get the joining-up age lowered – 'no lead for the little ones'; what a joke. But once on the Minos fast-track, the ammo, and the power, had been real. The SIG was light to carry and easy to fire. Felix had always seen his work as being about saving lives, not taking them; but if his own life was threatened, what choice did he have?

The responsibility felt awesome. His palms were sweating. He wondered how many people Sommers had slotted during his active service, and found he was glad to have a veteran on board for what might turn out to be his first firefight.

Sommers looked at him and smiled faintly. 'Bricking it, son?'

'A bit,' Felix admitted.

'Wouldn't be human if you weren't. But your training will take over. You'll be fine.'

'Sure we will,' said Hannah. But she said it as though she was trying to convince herself. She was dressed smartly in black trousers and top and had slapped some make-up on so she could get into the bar without drawing attention to herself; looking like a kid had its perks, but if you could look legal when you had to, you had the best of both worlds. She could easily have passed for eighteen.

As he fiddled listlessly with the straps of his rucksack, Felix saw that even Lili was sweating.

'You nervous too, sweetheart?' Sommers asked her. 'I wonder if Kanska's meeting with your replacement right now.' He held up his mobile phone, which showed a mugshot of Kanska from the ATLAS files – a bearded man in his thirties or forties with dark straggly hair. 'Imagine the looks on their faces when they find out you've led us straight to them. That'll pay Orpheus back for what they tried to do to you.'

Lili didn't respond, looking out over the wide, grey waters of the river Daugava. Felix held out a hand for the phone, looking into the heavy-lidded eyes of the wanted man staring back at him.

'My language tutor did tell me something about Riga's culture,' Hannah remarked, with a sideways look at Lili. 'Apparently, if you're passing this river and a fish sticks its head out and asks if Riga's finished, you have to answer "no". If you say yes, then Riga falls into the water.'

'Kanska's the one who'll be finished,' said Sommers.

'The translation is wrong,' Lili said quietly. 'It's "finished" as in "completed". And Orpheus's work will never be completed until your governments fall and your economy collapses.'

'And our people burn?' Felix felt a tingle in his spine. 'You still want that, don't you?'

'I don't care any more.' She looked away. 'I want to live.'

The taxi took them on into wide, leafy avenues. The architecture was beautiful but only the lines of the buildings were still clean; their fronts were tired and faded, paintwork peeling and bricks buried under grime. The evening sky held only a vestige of blue now, criss-crossed with a crazy cats' cradle of telegraph cables and overhead tram-wires.

As cobbled streets became a feature of the local geography, Sommers asked the taxi to take them to the Tornakalns railway station, up the road from their destination. Felix supposed it made sense to be discreet. Since Kanska was a big man and used this café as a regular haunt, it stood to reason he'd have lookouts. This way they could wander into the neighbourhood and just 'chance' upon the café-bar.

'Now,' Sommers went on, his craggy face a darker red than usual. 'We're all on the same page with the plan, yeah?'

'Kanska is our primary target,' said Hannah. 'If we get his lensmen too, so much the better.'

'And this briefing sounds big, there'll most likely be security,' Sommers said. 'Chances are the place is closed to the public. So, Felix . . . ?'

Felix swallowed. 'I go in round the back, take care of any guards and watch the exit, so Kanska can't run for it.'

'And I check out the front ahead of you and Lili,' Hannah told Sommers. 'If any guards stop me, I'll act like I thought I was meeting a friend there.'

'And while they're distracted, I'll take them,' Sommers said simply. 'Then Felix comes in from the back and we've got the bastards stuck in the middle.'

Lili looked at him anxiously. 'You'll take me with you?'

'You're going to identify everyone there for us,' Sommers told her. 'Now, come on. Let's do this.'

The four of them got out of the taxi and Lili surveyed the tired station building forlornly. As Hannah paid the cabbie and Felix secured his pack on his back, the big man cuffed one of Lili's wrists to his own.

She reacted with a look of outrage. 'I've helped you this far, haven't I?'

'Call me paranoid,' Sommers replied, stuffing her hand and his into his coat pocket. 'Shall we?'

The odd procession set off down the street, Sommers and Lili leading the way. No one spoke as they took the walkway beside a bridge across the railway tracks. Over the sound of the traffic Felix heard a low, tingling, rustling noise. He looked behind him and found an old blue-and-white tram sharing the tarmac and stonework as it trundled towards them. From here there was an amazing view across the Daugava river, to where the spires and steeples of Riga's indomitable churches stood gleaming. They felt to Felix a long way away from this part of town.

The tram bustled past, hissing and rattling. Felix adjusted the strap of his backpack and followed Hannah, Sommers and Lili across the bridge and onto a quiet, leafy street of once-grand wooden houses. One building stood out, made of brick and covered in plaster. There seemed no way in at street level but a metal-railed stone staircase led down out of sight.

'That's the café,' Lili whispered, holding back. 'It has no name. Those who know it, know it, those who do not, should not.'

Hannah's hand slipped subconsciously inside her jacket to cradle her gun. 'Good luck, everyone,' she murmured.

'Let's go,' Sommers said.

Felix separated from the group, detouring around the

side of the old house. The district seemed near deserted, which Felix was glad about. If things kicked off there would be fewer bystanders coming to harm, as well as fewer witnesses to whatever might happen.

As he rounded the corner, Felix pushed the cold sweaty anticipation of action to the back of his mind. He had to stay sharp. The back door of the café was ajar. No guards. How sloppy was that? Felix's heart was hammering hard enough to bruise as he pushed open the door. Inside it smelled musty. A utility room. The dull, dusty eye of a washing machine glared back at him. An old fridge hummed a strained monotone.

Felix heard the distant jangle of a bell; Hannah opening the door, he guessed. She'd taken care of security fast. Steeling himself, he stepped forward into the gloom of a short corridor. He saw scuffed lino and peeling, flowery wallpaper. A door marked 'Private' to his left.

Why no guards?

Felix tried the door. It opened onto a small, messy room with a desk buried under papers and empty glasses. Accounts. Invoices. He glanced at one – it listed drink deliveries for the month. Felix felt unease scratch at the back of his mind; this was clearly no big-shot terrorist's office.

Raised voices in Russian or Latvian sounded up ahead. Felix held his breath, then realized the exchange was being punctuated by suspenseful music. It was coming from a TV in the main bar. Creeping forward down the corridor to a set of saloon doors, he peered inside. The space was dark, lined with wood and cork, lit by dim bulbs in dusty shades and the flicker of the blaring TV. The bar was dead ahead of him and unmanned. The solitary barman was wiping down a table with his back turned to Felix – so Felix could see almost all of the café. It was nothing special. A few old men were drinking vodka or beer at wooden tables. Tough-looking guys in black leather sat with mobile phones clamped to their ears. And Hannah stood at the bar, waiting to be served. She caught his eye discretely.

No sign of Kanska.

Hannah looked around suddenly as though she'd lost something. She crossed back to the door, opened it – the bell above the door rang harshly – and pretended to scan the ground around the steps. Then she came back inside.

The signal, thought Felix, licking his dry lips.

As Hannah returned to the counter and the barman nodded to her to say he'd be there in a moment, the ragged chimes sounded again: Sommers pushed inside with Lili, coolly scanning the room. Felix noted that Lili was looking towards the back of the room, at something Felix couldn't quite see from his vantage point. She was biting her lip. Holding her breath.

Time slowed to a long, sharp second as Felix heard the creak of a door in the bar to his right. *Must be the door to the toilets*, he realized. Lili reacted. On instinct Felix stepped forward through the swinging doors into the space behind the bar. Now he could see a dark-suited man walking out from the gents', in aviator shades, a bunch of red roses in his hands, with something metal glinting through the thorn-spiked stalks.

'Stop! Put your hands in the air!' Felix yelled, pulling out his gun. But the man had pulled his gun from the bouquet at the same time and was a split second faster. He fired at Felix. Felix gasped as he was sent reeling into the back wall, smashing bottles and glasses with his pack as he crashed down to the floor. He felt no pain, only anger with himself that he had failed and shock that he was falling. *Where'd he get me? How bad?* Then Hannah was shouting something in Latvian or Russian over a sudden hubbub of babbling voices as more shots were fired off – two, three.

She fell silent. Sommers hadn't said a word.

Swearing under his breath, Felix struggled to rise. As he glanced to his left he found a bullet hole in the front of his rucksack visible over his shoulder – the bullet had barely missed him. Felix heard Lili's voice, high and frantic, and then another gunshot. Chase music swelled from the TV and the peal of the bell above the door sounded like laughter.

Felix crawled round from behind the bar, gun clutched in his trembling hand, in time to see Lili and Roses running up the steps from the café. Hannah was leaning on a table, her back to him, staring after them. Sommers lay on the floor, his eyes wide, a purple spot between them welling with blood. Felix felt his stomach turn. The man was dead, no question, and the handcuffs' chain, trailing from his wrist, had been broken with a close-range shot that had scorched the floorboards. 'Stop them!' Felix shouted at Hannah as he checked the rest of the room for further threats – the tough men in leathers were cowering under tables, the old men were eyeing Felix and his gun grimly, the barman was babbling but Felix couldn't understand a word. 'Come on, Hannah, what . . . ?'

Then with a jolt he saw she was shaking, and that blood was pooling at her feet. With a groan, she fell to her knees then toppled over onto her back. A bullet must have opened her stomach and her hands were clasped over a huge, scarlet stain.

Felix scrambled towards her. 'Hannah?' Her grey eyes looked glassily back at him as he pushed her knees up to lessen the strain on the wound. 'Stay with me, Hannah.'

'Get them,' she hissed faintly. 'Don't let them win.'

He tore off his hoodie and wrapped it round her middle, quickly sliding the sleeves under her back. He stared round at the bar, but only Sommers' dead gaze met his own. '*Vai jūs runajat angliski?*' Felix shouted. Hannah had taught him the phrase over coffee just that afternoon – *Does anyone here speak English?*

'Little,' wheezed one of the old men, his face pale.

'Call an ambulance. Give her first aid. You get me?' He tied the sleeves in a non-slip knot over her ribs, away from the wound, got up and ran to the door. 'Look after her or I'm coming back for you.' He checked the steps were clear and took them three at a time on trembling legs. *A come-on*, he thought blackly. *I knew it. A stinking come-on.*

He reached the pavement and stared around wildly, still stunned by the speed at which everything had gone to hell, trying to make sense of the situation. Had Kanska been tipped off they were coming and left a welcoming committee in his place? No, in that case he'd have made sure to execute the lot of them. Instead, Lili had been sprung. And that look in her eyes . . .

His mind worked its way around a rush of facts and supposition. Clearly Lili knew and cared for the man with the roses. If the two of them were friends or more from her time living here then it stood to reason Roses would share the same contacts and hear about the questions being asked. He could have bribed some of them to give this address and just wait for Lili to be delivered, ready to get her away at any cost.

'That cost's going to be higher than you think,' Felix muttered.

Still holding the gun, he straightened his rucksack over his shoulders and ran up onto the pavement. About a hundred metres away he saw Lili and Roses share a brief, fierce embrace in the spilled orange glare of a streetlamp before ducking into a white BMW 3-series saloon. So they weren't contacts or acquaintances, then. Lovers, escaping together into the night.

Felix tightened his grip on the gun. 'The hell you are . . .'

... SIXTEEN ...

Felix ran into the road as the BMW's engine roared, and took aim at the windscreen. But a man and a woman crossed the road, blocking his view. He ran forward desperately – but a blaring horn behind him made him turn and jump clear; a battered white van rumbled past, its driver shouting and gesturing. Felix took aim again, but now Roses was pulling away and Lili was pointing a pistol through the window. Swearing, Felix dived to the cobblestones as the gun went off. The passenger window of the Lada parked beside him shattered in a shower of brilliant shrapnel.

A young man opened the driver's door, a disbelieving 'what the hell?' look on his face as he shouted after the white saloon disappearing down the street. Felix jumped up, clocked the keys in the Lada's ignition. Not having to hotwire a motor would save precious moments. 'Speak

English?' he demanded. The man ignored him, so Felix opted for a more universal language and fired his gun in the air. 'I need your car!' The man blanched, turned and ran away. Then Felix saw a young woman cowering inside, her clothes dishevelled and lipstick smeared over her face. 'Get after him,' Felix told her, gesturing with the gun. 'Then kick his ass for leaving you alone.'

As the girl threw open the passenger door and ran, Felix thought of Hannah, abandoned and bleeding in the café. *I'm no better than that guy, running out on her*. But he knew that, like picking a Lada for a high-speed pursuit vehicle, he didn't have much choice. With a crunch of gears and a screeching wheelspin, Felix took the car out into the street. It was the first time he'd driven alone outside of the Moccas Court test track, despite passing the advanced driving course. But after the endless circuits he'd taken at ludicrous speeds, he felt confident enough, even with the driver's seat on the left.

Almost at once, a red Fiat rounded the corner and nearly totalled him, reminding Felix he needed to drive on the right over here. He swore – so much for confidence. But what the hell.

He floored the pedal in second gear, desperate to catch up with Lili and Roses. He was in luck. There were traffic lights ahead, stopped on red, and the Bimmer was waiting a couple of cars in front. Felix was about to jump out when the lights changed and Roses pulled away, careering recklessly up the street. Ignoring the honking horns around him, Felix did the same, swerving out into the oncoming traffic, cutting up the cars in his lane as he fought to keep the BMW in sight. Roses was swinging the powerful motor this way and that, cutting a swathe through the night-time traffic. Keeping up in a Lada wasn't going to be easy. Felix switched his satphone onto hands-free and speed-dialled the Minos hotline.

It was the Girl who answered. 'State your name and passcode.'

'Felix Smith. Passcode one-one-seven-nine. I'm pursuing Lili Vigas and accomplice in a white BMW registration Victor-Foxtrot-seven-three-one-Tango-X-ray out of the Tornakalns district of—'

'It's all right, Felix. I'm tracking you through your Minos chain.' She paused. 'We've been monitoring emergency service calls: an ambulance has been called for a white teenage female in—'

'Hannah and Sommers both shot,' Felix interrupted, accelerating into a bend, the wind biting in through the shattered window. 'Sommers is dead. Tonight was a come-on. I'm giving chase.' He paused. 'And incidentally, driving on real roads is freaking the hell out of me.' He accelerated through a changing red light to keep up with Roses. 'How come there are so many traffic lights?'

'We'll tap into Riga's CCTV network,' the Girl said calmly. 'See if we can spot you.'

The Bimmer took a sudden hard left, down a wide, well-appointed avenue into the oncoming traffic. A truck slammed on its brakes and skidded out of the way, lurching again as a van behind rammed into the back of it. Felix followed, the Lada's noisy engine rasping to a throaty crescendo as he took the corner – straight into the path of a motorbike dispatch rider. The bike veered away and mounted the pavement, smashing into a tobacconist's stall.

'Sorry,' Felix muttered, fighting to keep the white car in sight as it tore round another corner. He pumped the accelerator, depressed the clutch, then yanked up on the handbrake and twisted the wheel hard right, screeching into a street flanked by high-rise apartment buildings, overhead cables strung between them like black scratches on the sky. A big red truck was blocking the carriageway, as two men unloaded crates of drink into a convenience store. A tanker was blocking the opposite lane so Roses had no choice but to slow down and wait for it to pass, allowing Felix precious seconds to catch up. He aimed his gun through the window and fired off a volley of deliberate shots, the recoil shaking through his arm. The Bimmer's boot took two hits, the windscreen shattered under a third, but its wheels were already spinning as Roses pulled out and darted around the red truck, hanging a right almost immediately to get out of firing range.

'Felix?' the Girl's voice sounded over the phone speaker. 'It looks like your target's heading for the river.'

'Not the airport then,' Felix muttered. 'Someplace else.'

He sent the Lada skidding round the corner in pursuit and felt the car tyres bump over tracks in the road – tramlines. There was a tram gliding towards them – and Roses was accelerating head-on, fixed on a collision course.

Felix yelled out loud in frustration. He couldn't fire again and risk hitting the tram. And he knew that as a result, Roses would only swerve out of the tram's path at the last moment. *But which way will he jump?* The tram was already squealing noisily to a halt, but the BMW was still coming. Felix kept his heel on the accelerator, drawing closer to the car, the tram, to the mother of all collisions. 'Turn!' he shouted, gripping the wheel so hard his knuckles cracked. 'Turn, you son of a—'

At the last second Felix bottled it and steered hard to the right – just as Roses swung a left. Felix stamped down on the brake and shifted into first, brought the Lada steaming to an emergency stop. But now the tram had come to a halt too, the battered blue-and-white carriages blocking his path. Felix reversed rapidly, rear-ending a parked Mercedes as he did so, then turned the wheel and screeched away from the stalled tram, back in pursuit. There was a side street off to the left that Roses must have taken, and Felix screamed round into it.

'Half a dozen police cars are heading your way, Felix,' the Girl warned him. 'And a traffic-cam's picked up a white BMW heading for the big Southern Bridge. Damage to the rear windows but different registration from the one you gave me.'

'Lili's knight in shining armour must've rigged the plates somehow,' Felix realized. 'So it's me the cops are going to come after.' He wanted to smash the steering wheel but forced himself to stay calm. Just as he was about to hightail it away, he noticed the hazards on a parked silver Lexus flash twice behind him, and saw a greying businessman stride out into the road, ready to get in. Felix stomped on the brake, ground the gearstick into reverse and sent the Lada hurtling backwards once again. But this time he opened the driver's door a little as he passed the Lexus and clipped the man, just enough to bruise and knock him to the floor, no more. Then, grabbing his pack and phone, Felix de-bussed and threw open the door of the Lexus. He dumped his stuff in the passenger seat and swapped the keys from the dazed businessman's hand for a 500-lati note by way of apology. Then he turned the key in the ignition and pulled away with a little more finesse. It would take a few minutes for the police to work out which car they ought to chase now.

But how was he ever going to catch up to Lili and Roses? *How they must be gloating. They think they've got away with it. A tidy old night.*

'Target's on the bridge, Felix,' the Girl said abruptly. 'Turn right at the end of this road and follow the sign for *Dienvidu Tilts*.'

'On it,' Felix told her, switching on the Lexus's built-in satnav. As he searched for the English language option, he swallowed. 'Any word on Hannah?'

The Girl paused too. 'Nothing yet. We're working on it. Meantime, get Lili back.'

Felix said nothing, inputting the name of the bridge on the satnav touchscreen while accelerating into sixth gear. He hammered through the increasingly drab and industrial streets close to the river, past superstores and ceramics factories. The bright orange pylons and cables that held the Southern Bridge above the Daugava came into sight, a spaghetti-junction swirl of asphalt and concrete guarding the approach. A virtual version appeared on the satnav screen at the same time.

'Speed camera's picked up your target along *Maskavas Iela* – that's Moscow Street,' the Girl reported. 'They could turn off at any moment to get to any one of the residential areas and go to ground; if they do, finding them will be next to impossible—'

'I said I'm on it.' As Felix drove onto the bridge, he checked the satnav map for Moscow Street – and started as he recognized a place name close by. 'Kengarags,' he breathed, thinking aloud. 'Lili said she used to live there with a friend. What if that friend was Roses? Even if not, she might still have stuff in the friend's flat, money or things she needed—'

'Say again?'

'Kengarags. It's possible they're making for there.'

'I'll see what I can find.'

Felix floored the pedal, hope giving fresh urgency to the chase. The bright yellow streetlights glared down at him in pairs. The orange support struts and cables were like giant half-spun webs against the darkening charcoal of night. He swung in and out of the three lanes of traffic – *getting the hang of this, now* – before zigzagging off to an exit and following the mannered English directions towards Moscow Street. The river was to his right now, wide and dark. A forbidding landscape of dilapidated buildings and drab concrete apartment blocks slowly took root around him.

'No sign,' the Girl reported.

Even if they are here, how'm I ever going to find

them, Felix thought bitterly. *One flat in amongst all these—*

A roiling flower of incandescent flame burst from one of the apartment buildings to his left, and a thundering boom hollowed out the night. 'No way,' Felix whispered. 'Another IED?'

Guess I just found them.

. . . FIFTEEN . . .

Swinging the wheel, Felix swerved across three lanes, smashed through a row of traffic cones and abandoned the Lexus on the pavement beside a low concrete wall. A ghastly feeling of calm settled over him as he cleared his stuff from the passenger seat. The chase was over now. No escape for Lili. She had been marked for death. Orpheus clearly hadn't been fooled by Zane's misdirection to Bulgaria. They'd known ATLAS were taking Lili here. And they must've known too that she – or ATLAS investigators – would surely check out her place in Riga, and so arranged a little welcoming present.

But Felix had to be sure. Grunting with effort, his heavy pack weighing him down, he propelled himself over the wall into the grounds of the commie block. The flames gusting from the empty third-floor windows cast a hellish red tint over the unkempt gardens, warming the battered white of the Bimmer parked clumsily outside. People were starting to gather, some huddling together for comfort while others ran with children clutched to their chests, yelling and shouting.

Felix studied the shattered windows and stonework as black smoke fled the flames to be as one with the night. Could there be a secondary IED waiting to detonate up there, as there had been back on the estate? Someone might be watching, waiting for Lili's pursuer to enter the building so they could take him out too . . .

'Back!' he shouted at the transfixed crowds, trying to warn them away. 'Get back!' They ignored him, of course, couldn't understand his language; and anyway, to them he was just a kid.

More smoke belched out from inside and engulfed the onlookers. With all views of the entrance obscured, Felix took his chance and ran inside the blazing building. If there was a secondary and the bomber was watching out for a bomb disposal team, he would hardly be expecting a lone teenager.

Yeah, Minos had been set up with good reason, Felix decided. He'd prove that.

There were people shambling down the steps, whether drunk or in shock, Felix couldn't tell. He pushed past them, took his respirator from his backpack and fixed it in place. As he neared the third floor he could feel the heat on his skin, and smoky air crackling in his lungs. The stench of petrol and roasting flesh was enough to make him gag as he pushed open the fire door leading from the stairwell and entered the communal landing.

It was a wreck of concrete debris. In here, the smoke hung in the air like malevolent spirits. A young woman stumbled past Felix, sobbing and moaning; half her hair had burned away, exposing a raw, sticky scalp. He turned automatically to help her through the door to the steps, then noticed a charred body sprawled against the wall opposite the gaping doorway of the blasted apartment. Felix saw the twisted frames of a pair of dark glasses, welded onto the corpse's blackened head, and his stomach turned. *Rest in pieces, Roses.*

Another figure lay slumped further along the corridor, shaking and twitching in the rubble, a bloodied mess. Felix almost puked as he saw what was left of Lili. With all the smoke he couldn't tell which limbs had been crushed by concrete and which blown clear away. But she was alive, staring at him with ash-laced eyes. 'Help me,' she croaked. 'I want to live.'

So did Hannah, he wanted to scream in her face. But he bit back his anger. He knew he should check first for secondaries in the apartment, but could Lili last that long?

Taking a chance, he ran over to her, assessed her condition and quickly saw there was little he could do. Her wounds were too massive and too many; the concrete crushing her body was all that was holding her together.

'Henri . . .' She gestured down the landing at Roses' body with the claw-like remains of one hand. 'He's OK?'

Felix thought of the charred corpse behind him and closed his watering eyes. There was no sense in telling Lili the truth. 'He'll make it to hospital.' An idea struck him. 'But first, you have to tell us everything you know.'

Her eyes narrowed. 'You promise you'll help him?'

Felix chose his words carefully. 'He'll get all the help he needs – *if* you talk. Deal?'

Lili scowled. 'Henri was working with Kanska but wanted out. We were quitting . . . Starting again . . . Just us. I was going to fly out and meet Henri at the airport.'

Felix frowned. 'The air ticket to Riga in your room . . . There never was a big briefing planned, was there? You just let us *think* that. And when we started asking about a meeting, Henri saw to it that we got one.'

'I'd already been briefed,' Lili admitted. 'By Rashed. He set me up with the place in London.'

Felix leaned in closer. 'That diagram – you know what it means, don't you?'

But Lili's eyes were losing whatever focus they had. 'Henri had tickets for South America.' Blood leaked from her split lips as she choked on the evil smoke. 'In the car I *told* him we should forget the evidence, just get straight to the airport . . .'

'Evidence?' Felix leaned closer. 'What evidence?'

'Henri recorded what Orpheus were doing. Insurance, he called it.' Her blackened eyes filled with bloody tears. 'He just told me that Kanska found out about it and sent Rashed to get me, in case I was keeping it in the flat . . .'

'It was evidence against Kanska?' Felix tried to take her hand, but she cried out with pain.

'Heat,' she breathed, her eyes flickering shut. 'Warm air . . .'

'That's the fire,' he told her. 'Stay with me, Lili. Tell me about the evidence. What's the job Orpheus are planning? Where's it going to happen?'

'Test . . . test driving . . .' Her eyes stayed shut, her words were slurring. 'Tunnel . . . Root out Irbil . . .'

'I don't understand you,' Felix said frantically. He thumbed at her sticky black eyelids, trying to open them. 'Come on! What were you supposed to be filming? That diagram of the tower blocks, what does it mean?'

'Tower blocks . . .' She sounded delirious, shaking her head. 'You won't see . . . Mine . . . On the ground.'

'What mine?' Felix flinched as she threw back her head, writhing in silent agony. 'Lili, what do you mean?' But as he stared helplessly down at her, she stopped struggling. He knew she was dead.

Rising without a word, trembling with shock, Felix turned back to the apartment. The heat was incredible, but if that evidence was still inside . . .

He stepped back into the ruined front room, replacing his respirator, and forced himself to focus, searching swiftly and systematically through the flames and debris for secondary IEDs as well as whatever dirt Henri might have had on Orpheus. What traps had been left for the disposal team who would inevitably follow? One triggered by laser-sights would already have detonated as shrapnel from the first blast crossed the laser beam . . . So, a remote-activated IED? Felix shuddered. He'd defeated one with the ECM jammer before, so he decided to employ that little gadget again, just in case the bomber was sticking to his tried and tested technique. But as he placed the jammer on the floor, he saw something small and disc-shaped lodged under a slab of concrete.

It looked to be an anti-personnel mine – an MS3, pressure-release. Felix shuddered despite the baking heat. So it was this that Lili had been warning him about – *You won't see mine on the ground*. Lifting the concrete removed the weight from the pressure plate, which in turn   released the mine's striker and – *boom*. The three hundred grams of TNT packed inside tore you apart.

Crude as booby traps go, he thought, *but in conditions like this, it could well have been effective.*

He couldn't defuse it safely here, and he had to move fast. So he gave the area a wide berth and searched on . . . Nothing in the kitchen . . . nothing in the living room . . .

The smoke was getting thicker, and the ceiling was beginning to collapse. It was getting harder to see anything at all. Then, in the remains of a bedroom, through the splintered skeleton of a futon, Felix saw a buckled grate set into the wall. *And another of Lili's mutterings suddenly makes sense*, he realized. It was part of the block's warm-air heating system. Something metal glinted behind it. Henri's evidence? Or bait left by the bomber who'd already nicked it?

Crossing quickly, Felix studied the area, deemed it clear of threat, unscrewed the grate and tugged out a scorched metal toolbox. It felt searing hot even through his protective gloves as he wrestled the lid open. There were several DVDs inside, some fused to their plastic cases and ruined, all unmarked. Surely here was the evidence Orpheus had hoped to destroy . . .

Felix jumped as a section of the wall fell behind him with a creaking crash. As he turned, a high-pressure jet of water as thick as a neck exploded in through the flame-cloaked windows, and suddenly the air was liquid with steam and soot. The fire brigade was here. *If they manage to dislodge that concrete slab . . .*

Frantically, the box under one arm and his rucksack over his shoulder, Felix sprinted out of the flat. A second after he'd cleared the front doorway, a tremendous explosion shook him off his feet and lethal fragments embedded themselves in the wall of the communal corridor.

It could've been redecorated with my lower body, Felix realized shakily. But at least now the mine was neutralized.

He jammed the respirator and toolbox into his ruck-sack and walked quickly if a little unsteadily to the stairwell. Firefighters were picking their way towards him, and one immediately broke away to help him back down the stairs to the fresher air outside. He thought of Hannah's uncle fighting the flames at Day Zero, dying so others could get away. Once outside, Felix gripped the man's hand tightly in thanks before letting him vanish back inside the building.

His eyes were running with the smoke. He wished they were tears – tears for Hannah or for Sommers, or for Lili even. Something to show his heart could be touched by more than fear and fury. But there was nothing behind his eyes, and only a hard kernel of anger in his chest.

Police cars and ambulances were arriving. The bomb squad would doubtless be turning up soon. Felix made his way unobtrusively to the white BMW his bullets had ventilated. Henri's car. He quickly got inside and searched it for anything incriminating, but all he found was a battered bouquet of red roses on the back seat. Felix picked them up as he left the car. There were thirteen blooms.

An even number is only for funerals, Lili had said.

He plucked out one of the roses and crushed it in his fist. Then he tossed the rest to the muddy ground and took off on foot without a backward look.

... FOURTEEN ...

The next morning was bright and cool. The sun stared down at Felix from a bald white sky. He sat alone on a bench on Freedom Boulevard, a wide-open pedestrianized plaza just beyond the Old Town. Locals hurried by, while tourists lingered. The silent waters of a canal stretched behind him, dark as his thoughts.

Last night had proved a busy one.

He'd risked going back to his hotel for a change of clothes but hadn't dared stay. He was certain he'd be recognized – after threatening the couple in the car at gunpoint and stealing their wheels his description would soon be all over Riga.

Hannah's words had echoed back to him: *Never heard of hiding in plain sight?*

She was still critical in hospital. Felix had tried to get to her and see she was OK, but a heavy police presence made the whole area a no-go. He wondered where Sommers' body was being kept. If the man's family and friends had any idea yet what had gone down. Felix felt numb. He couldn't stop picturing the bullethole in Sommers' head. The unseeing eyes. The blood. The silence.

His first time up close with a corpse.

'Pull through, Hannah,' he whispered, rubbing his eyes. 'You've got to.'

Felix played the night's dark movements over again in his mind. He'd ditched his backpack in a skip on a building site. At the hotel, he'd called in to a mostly silent Zane and given his report on the miniature apocalypse he'd lived through, made arrangements for a meet. Zane had told him to get to a late-night chemist where he could buy black hair-dye and fake tan to darken his appearance. That achieved, back out on the streets, Felix had spotted a man on a stag party discard his pair of 'comedy breasts', and moved in to claim them for his own. *Dangerous fugitives don't normally go around wearing big plastic bosoms*, he'd reasoned. They also don't tend to show them off in busy tourist spots. Which was why he'd been sitting for hours on a bench with his head in his hands, like someone bitterly regretting the night before.

True enough.

Felix rubbed his tired eyes. He might look like a different person, but right now, he wished he really was one. Zane was due to meet him in a hotel in Riga at midday, check over the evidence he'd acquired and hopefully get him the hell out of here. Someone at Minos was already working with Latvian authorities to clear up the mess with minimum fuss. A cover story about drug barons caught in a gunfight with two teenage dealers was being prepared – and as minors, Hannah and Felix's details would be kept out of the press. *'Nothing happened here, move along.'* Sommers would be shipped home quietly in a box and Hannah would be moved back to Britain once she came out of intensive care. If she could just keep holding on . . .

Felix stared blankly at the changing of the guard beside the Freedom Monument, a great granite spindle mounted on a carved plinth, crowned with a copper figurine holding three stars aloft – one for each of the principalities of Latvia. The monument represented freedom for a country that had been occupied by other powers for all but fifty years of its 800-year history. Perhaps that explained why Latvian soldiers stepped so delicately about it as the ceremony proceeded – tread too hard and the whole thing might come crashing down around their ears.

Freedom is so fragile, Felix brooded. People of all different lands and cultures had fought and died for it throughout history, and yet what did it even mean? One man's freedom fighter was another man's terrorist. People like Lili, like Henri, Kanska and all the rest, they no doubt saw themselves as legitimate combatants in a struggle to destroy a culture they saw as corrupt. And since they hadn't sufficient numbers to win in open combat, acts of terror were their instruments of war. The 'propaganda of the deed', a means to bring about political change through intimidation, destruction and wholesale slaughter.

In the wake of Day Zero, it sometimes felt as though the only freedom was the freedom to live in fear.

'But we'll go on fighting,' Felix muttered.

He eyed the sculptured figures around the base of the monument: soldiers and priests. Mothers and children. Slaves breaking free of their chains.

Felix felt a little better when Zane showed at the Hotel Amrita, a modern, glass-fronted building at odds with the old-fashioned mansions around it.

'Nice rack you have there,' Zane remarked wryly in the lift to the top floor. 'Part of the new look, huh?'

'Oh . . .' Felix self-consciously scooped off the scuffed plastic as they entered Zane's room. 'I'd forgotten I was wearing them.' He emptied out a charred selection of mini DV tapes and DVDs from the cups. 'They've been keeping the evidence warm.'

Zane studied the melted casing of one cassette. 'Looks like it got warm enough already.' He reached into his pocket and passed Felix a new passport and driving licence. 'Here.' They showed his name to be Mitchell, and the photo on each had been digitally altered to give him dark hair and a tan. 'To go with your new look.'

'Thanks,' said Felix without much feeling. 'I'll get used to it in maybe twenty years or so.'

'We're making sure your police description is taken out of circulation.' Zane pulled out his laptop and slotted one of Henri's DVDs inside. 'A few handshakes in high places, we'll pay some compensation to your car-crime victims and it'll be like nothing ever happened.'

Felix couldn't quite muster the energy for a hollow laugh.

'Hey.' Zane looked at him. 'I know it wasn't easy out there, your first firefight and all. You did well.'

'If I'd done better, Sommers and Hannah wouldn't be where they are now.' Felix slumped down on the bed. 'I doubt the tapes and discs will even play. I tried them. Too scorched or scratched or something.'

'Our tech guys should be able to scrape some data out of them,' Zane said. 'I'll just run a utility check on this one . . .'

Felix nodded. 'Did . . . did you see Hannah?'

'Her condition's still critical,' Zane remarked, opening a bag of crisps as he tapped at the buzzing laptop. 'Damn shame. You think maybe she got herself shot on purpose so she could hassle any passing guys for the kiss of life?'

Felix stayed quiet. He supposed Zane's making light of things was just his way of dealing with it. 'Who was this Henri guy, anyway?' he asked, changing the subject. 'Any positive ID?'

'Henri Talhami,' Zane declared. 'Known former associate of our radioactive bomber friend, Fenar Rashed. Worked on the fringes of professional terrorism most of his life, most recently as a tunnel operator in Rafah, smuggling weapons under the Gaza Strip between Egypt and Palestine.' He snorted. 'If he'd ever switched to our side he'd have been right behind Minos. The smugglers use plenty of kids to help build their tunnels. To them, it's cheap and disposable labour.'

Felix considered. 'Hope Minos don't see us that way.'

Zane typed in a series of passwords, logging on to the internet. 'The amount of training we've given you, you think you're cheap?'

At that, Felix found a smile. 'Guess not.' He paused. 'Had Henri been messing about with radiation, like Rashed?'

'His blood cells show traces.' Zane crunched thoughtfully on another big mouthful. 'Speaking of Rashed, we've found where he was holed up, thanks to a couple of Minos agents hanging tough with that kidult gang that he paid to beat up on Hannah. They got us the lead. And it turns out Rashed had transformed a bedsit in Staines into a nice little bomb factory. Undoubtedly where he built the devices you defused in Northolt. First crack at forensics suggests those IEDs that trashed Cardiff and Birmingham back in the spring were built there too.'

'Wish we'd got him alive,' Felix muttered. 'Learned what else he was planning, what this job that Kanska's setting up is all about.'

'Me too,' Zane agreed. 'We found plans and photos there of a dozen major cities worldwide and several more here in the UK.'

'Targets,' Felix breathed. '*Multiple* targets? Could Orpheus be planning some kind of international strike?'

Zane shrugged. 'We've got agents checking out other known associates of Rashed. But it's taking time.' He wiped salt from his lips. 'Anyways, with luck there's something on these discs that'll show us how his butt got radioactive. Maybe even a clue to where Kanska's hiding out now.'

'I can't believe how well Lili and Henri played us,' Felix murmured. 'The whole thing was a dead end.'

'Be grateful to Henri.' Zane started typing again. 'His "insurance" is our only lead to what Orpheus are planning.'

Felix remembered Lili's last whispered words. 'Test-driving tunnel . . . Root out Irbil. New something or other.' He sighed. 'What was she on about?'

'Doesn't sound like she was just raving,' Zane weighed in. 'She warned you about the mine and she was right – right? So we've got to find out what the hell else she was on about.' He stuffed the last of the crisps into his mouth and tossed the empty packet on the floor. 'Orpheus are going a long way to protect their upcoming surprise. Only one conclusion you can draw – it's gonna be big and bad. Bigger than Day Zero.'

'The grand opening of New Heathrow?' Felix mused. 'Kill the PM, the royals, about a thousand VIPs . . .' He shook his head. 'They should never have rebuilt that airport. It's going to be, like, a terrorist magnet.'

'In terms of international passenger traffic Heathrow was the world's busiest airport. It's needed.' Zane shot him a sharp look. 'Besides, you think we should just roll over and let them take from us? Never make a stand?'

'I . . .' Felix shook his head. 'No. Of course not.'

'I know Heathrow's an extra-touchy subject for you,' Zane murmured. 'If it makes you feel any better, in addition to just about the tightest security anywhere in the world, we're remote scanning the entire area for IEDs on a daily basis, including aerial searches for the tiniest whiff of explosive vapour. And so far, fat zilch. And speaking of zilch, the sketch of the tower blocks doesn't line up with anything in the area. Of course, if it's just one part of the diagram, we need to lay hands on the other pieces of the picture.'

Felix nodded. 'You're checking the wreckage of Lili and Henri's flat?'

'Naturally. Though it's one hell of a mess.' Zane sighed. 'In the meantime, in light of the new evidence at Rashed's bedsit, we're widening the search to take in other major cities around the globe. As you say, if there are multiple targets . . .'

'Then we're really stuffed,' Felix muttered. 'It's the old story, isn't it? The terrorists only have to be lucky once. We have to be lucky always.' He held his head in both hands. 'And we have to find Kanska.'

'Got the tera-heads working on it twenty-four seven. They're looking internationally, wading through CCTV footage of stations, airports – hell, just about everywhere.' Zane nodded. 'And we're working our way through Lili's contacts, shaking up each and every one for anything they can tell us. We'll find that son of a bitch. We've got to.'

'But we need to find him *fast*.' Felix puffed out a deep breath. '"Root out Irbil," she said. That's Irbil in Iraq, right? Could mean, root out a traitor? Or a route out of Irbil?'

Zane nodded. 'Or you misheard her and she said, "Rotate a gerbil."'

The two of them laughed, easing the tension.

'There is one weird thing about Irbil,' Zane went on thoughtfully. 'A remote Kurdish village a few miles outside it was pretty much wiped off the map last year. Razed to the ground. No survivors.'

'Ethnic cleansing or something?'

'No one came forward to claim responsibility. And there's no hard evidence as to what caused it – or why it was a target in the first place. But get this. A local construction firm cleared away the debris before official investigation could even begin. A firm whose name appears on no official paperwork.'

Felix sucked in his cheeks. 'And you think Orpheus have something to do with that blitzed village in Irbil?'

'Something that links to whatever they're planning now,' said Zane. 'Maybe it was a test exercise? I don't know.'

Silence stewed the air in the hotel room.

'So, what happens next?' Felix asked suddenly. 'Will the military send troops out to Irbil, try to pick up on whatever Orpheus leads might be waiting there?'

'Not an option,' Zane said simply. 'You know the UK and US have withdrawn troops from Iraq. We can't just send in forces to secure the area, especially when we don't even know what we're looking for. And besides, no one knows better than you how quickly and decisively Orpheus has acted to eradicate anything or anyone that could compromise this operation. A strong military presence – even ATLAS agents snooping about – could tip them off and do a whole lot more harm than good.'

Felix nodded. 'But if a lone agent could get into Irbil undetected, and carry out a low-key investigation . . .'

'Ideally a kid. 'Cause who'd expect a kid to take on a job like that?' Zane scowled and sighed. 'There's this big Iraqi medical university in Irbil; it runs exchange pro- grammes with other universities in the US and Europe. In two days' time, a group of first-year Turkish students are travelling there by coach for a week of lectures from some international healthcare experts.'

'I can't pass myself off as an eighteen-year-old Turkish student! I can't even speak the language . . .' Even as he spoke, Felix realized the score. 'You had Hannah down for the job, didn't you?'

'Right.' Zane nodded. 'But events have kind of got in the way of that little plan, haven't they?'

Felix could feel himself start to sweat. 'So what happens instead?'

'I don't want this Irbil tip-off going elsewhere,' Zane said, his voice growing a little harder. 'The lead came to Minos and we're holding onto it. A big, visible win is what the Chapter needs, Felix, to silence all those doubters in GI5 who voted against us recruiting minors.'

'Politics, huh?' A tingle of anticipation crawled through Felix's bones. 'So what's going to happen?'

'I can't pull anyone else onto this one with things so hot. You're all I've got right now.' Zane smiled grimly. 'And if you're the guy I think you are, you'll soon get past the shakes that last night gave you and be wanting to see this assignment through. Whatever it takes?'

Felix nodded slowly. 'All the way.'

'Good. A tera-head will be in touch soon to discuss your itinerary.' Zane slapped a big hand down on Felix's shoulder and smiled suddenly. 'Man, I envy you, you know that? I hear northern Iraq is just beautiful this time of year.'

... THIRTEEN ...

Felix killed the rest of the day on his hotel bed, surfing the web and watching the scraps of footage salvaged so far by ATLAS techies – the so-called evidence for which Henri and Lili had been executed.

I really do need to get a life, he thought. *Or would that make me less ready to risk my own?*

On first viewing there seemed little worth watching through the digital dropouts and stuttering images. Car parks and building sites. Craters in the ground. A gloomy tunnel with a filthy tarpaulin flapping down from its ceiling, concealing whatever lay on the other side. A man who might have been Kanska, looking way older than his mug shot, drinking and laughing in a bar someplace with other men, one of whom was surely Fenar Rashed. According to the experts, this bar was in Irbil.

Part of the footage showed two lorries parked back to

back with men unloading one to stack up the other. The nature of the cargo was unclear but it was swathed in tarpaulins and clanked like metal – scaffolding poles or other building materials? Both lorries looked pretty nondescript, unmarked and well-used. Then someone was led out of the lorry, half covered in a blanket. It could've been Rashed, but it was hard to be sure as the footage scuzzed up a moment later.

'Route out . . . Irbil,' Felix murmured. Had Orpheus been trafficking terrorists into Britain, hidden in the backs of lorries? Was that how Rashed had showed up on Lili's estate without anyone knowing?

Whatever's useful in Henri's clip collection, I guess ATLAS will find it. He put the computer to sleep and thought about joining it. It was late, and he was bushed.

Then his satphone trilled loudly and set his heart skipping. He answered quickly.

'It's me,' said the Girl.

'Name and password,' Felix shot at her.

'Funny.' She paused. 'You know, you're going on quite a journey.'

'You sound like a fortune teller.'

'Tomorrow at zero-five-thirty hours, a car will take you to Riga International Airport where you'll catch a commercial flight to Istanbul. From there you'll take a connecting flight to Erkilet International Airport in Kayseri. Your cover story is that your dad's a contractor for a Turkish IT consultancy and you're joining him for a short stay.'

Felix frowned. 'Won't I stand out, a fifteen-year-old flying on my own?'

'Most airlines let kids as young as five travel alone, so long as they're registered for the Unaccompanied Minors service,' the Girl informed him. 'Over the age of fourteen, with very few exceptions, you're considered a young adult and generally no restrictions apply. It's actually an advantage as you'll be fast-tracked through customs.'

'What about my pack? Kit? Pistol?'

'You'll be met at Erkilet Airport by a man named Chuck, Thursday at noon. He'll supply you with new equipment and transport you to the Iraqi border after an overnight stop in Diyarbakir, the largest city in south-eastern Turkey. He'll take you forward to the border early the next morning. But from there you must make entry to Iraq alone.'

'Cross-country?'

'I think your love for running has been noted,' the Girl said wryly. 'Only this time run like the devil's on your back. This crossing over the mountains will be dangerous.'

'Do you mean the terrain or the locals?'

'Both. Your presence will be entirely unofficial and, like all Minos operations, completely deniable if necessary to preserve the Chapter's secret status.'

Felix heaved a sigh. 'So I'm on my own.'

'You will have your satphone,' she reminded him. 'In line with operator etiquette, you must call in at regular intervals.'

'Every two minutes,' Felix joked darkly.

'Once in Iraq, make for the town of Dahuk. We'll give you co-ordinates and a time to rendezvous with a taxi driver named Abdul-Rahim. He'll take you to Irbil and assist in your search for evidence of Kanska's activities.'

'Well,' Felix reflected, 'if it has to be done, I guess sneaking in the back way's the safest option, right? Orpheus could have access to Border control records – and after what happened here and back on Lili's estate, they may have visual on me. My disguise is pretty awesome, but it might not fool them.'

'That's part of the reason. But mainly we just like to piss you off.'

Her words coaxed a nervous laugh out of him. 'What's the truth about what you do?' he asked. 'You're a lot more than just admin and logistics, aren't you, tera-head?'

There was silence for a few moments on the other end of the line. 'You guessed,' she said, a teasing note to her voice. 'Really, I'm here just for you, Felix.'

'I knew it.' Felix smoothed a hand over his rumpled bedsheets. 'How were you selected for Minos? You know everything about me, why can't I know about—?'

'Do you feel you know what you're doing yet?' she interrupted.

'Sorry?'

'The first thing you said to me when we met – "To be honest, I don't know what I'm doing." '

Felix raised his eyebrows, leaned back on the bed. 'Well, to *still* be honest, I don't remember that.'

'*I* do. I remember everything.' She sighed. 'Tera-heads aren't just here to spout air travel timetables at you. We each have an eidetic memory – total recall of images, sounds and objects.'

'That's a whole other level of data retrieval,' Felix murmured. 'Remind me never to lie in front of a tera-head.'

'It wouldn't be wise,' she agreed.

'It's kind of a gift you have.'

'Some think so. We all have our part to play. You seem quite gifted yourself – with luck if nothing else.'

'Are all tera-heads young?'

'I'm the youngest. We're an ATLAS resource, not exclusively Minos, so the same age-limits don't apply.' She paused. 'I suppose they put me onto Minos because I happen to be fifteen.'

Felix smiled. 'We're the same age.'

'I'm older.'

'Congratulations.'

'Thanks.'

Felix held on the line in silence for a few seconds. 'I probably don't,' he said at last.

'I'm sorry?' the Girl asked.

'To answer your question, I probably don't know what I'm doing yet.'

'You're fighting in a war,' said the Girl. 'Don't lose sight of that, Felix. Not once, not ever. Not for one split second. And come back to us alive.' A note of what might have been humour crept into her voice. 'After all, you did tell me we would prove the critics wrong about life expectancy in Minos.'

He thought of Hannah and Sommers. 'I really don't know much, do I?'

'You'll know more when you're back from Irbil,'

the Girl said. 'Keep us updated as to your progress.'

'You know it.' He hesitated. 'So long, then. Remember me.'

'That's my job, Felix.' After the tiniest of pauses, she hung up.

Felix put down the phone and half smiled. 'That, and maybe boosting morale for the guy without a life.'

He switched off the light and lay wakeful in the dark, watching the glowing red numbers on the clock-radio blink and change, ticking off time till the taxi arrived and the biggest challenge of his life began.

... TWELVE ...

'Time to wake up, son. We're almost there.'

Felix woke at the sound of Chuck's deep, mellifluous voice and checked the clock in the Jeep's dashboard. The former US Navy SEAL had been driving Felix across Turkey for nine uneventful hours. But though the Turkish landscape was amazing, it had barely scratched Felix's eyeballs. He was too busy wondering what lay ahead, and counting the knots in his tightening stomach.

Looking around, he realized that at last they were now deep into the south of the country, entering Diyarbakir's ancient city gates. The Byzantine city wall that stretched for miles in each direction looked dark and foreboding, reflecting the mood of the people; there had been fierce clashes between the local Kurdish population and Turkish security forces for several days now. The PKK – Kurdistan Workers' Party – was the best-known of the terrorist organizations seeking to win greater rights for Kurds in Turkey through violence, but there were others too.

Everywhere's a war zone, thought Felix. *Including my head.* He'd been travelling for ages, and exhaustion was kicking in big-time. His flight to Kayseri had landed at noon as planned, but he'd barely caught it; his night-flight from Riga to Istanbul had been delayed for hours.

'*Never mind*,' the smiley stewardess told him. '*You've got your dad's big wedding to look forward to when you arrive.*'

'*Yeah, it's gonna be sweet*,' Felix said sourly.

Now Chuck pulled up outside a cheap hotel near the slums to the west, one favoured by backpackers, and leaped out of the Jeep. He was a tall, lean man, blond and blue-eyed behind his aviator shades. He opened Felix's door, helped him out, then passed him the large holdall that had been on the back seat for the entire journey. Then the two of them checked in and headed for their rooms.

'How does this stopover fit with the cover story?' Felix wondered.

'Let's see.' Chuck shrugged. 'I'm your dad's best man, looking after you. Stag-night stunt went wrong; he wound up in the back of a lorry heading to Iraq and was only discovered at the border. We're collecting him from the jailhouse.'

Felix considered. 'How plausible.'

'Damn sight likelier than a lot of the crap that goes down round here,' Chuck remarked, opening the door with a waft of fetid air. 'Be ready to leave again at oh-two-thirty hours. Don't drink the water. I wouldn't touch the food, either. Not unless you want your butt spitting brown water all the next day.'

'Nice thought,' Felix rejoined, as Chuck's door shut behind him.

Once inside his own grotty hotel room, Felix took out his pocket radio-frequency detector and expertly swept the place for bugs. It was clean.

Then, in time-honoured, nerve-soothing style, he began unpacking his rucksack, acquainting himself properly with its contents. Inside it there was a holdall containing a GPS, laptop, camera, DSL modem and a G36K assault rifle with ten magazines of ammunition. Beneath it had been placed a 'grab bag' full of emergency kit containing clothing, basic medical supplies, a twenty-four-hour ration pack and the by now familiar SIG 229 automatic pistol. On top of that he had all his usual bomb-breaking kit. It weighed nearly as much as the rock-filled packs he'd shouldered on Steel-Buns Fawcett's mountain speed marches.

Felix smiled sadly to himself. He'd spent the whole three months impatiently wishing to leave, to get on with his active service. Now, within days of leaving, he found the pangs of nostalgia for his time at Moccas were as sharp as hunting knives. Sometimes, just now and then, he'd caught himself wondering if Private Pete was the lucky one for failing selection . . .

'Stop feeling so sorry for yourself,' he said out loud. 'It's adapt or die. And you're going to adapt.'

He quickly checked everything was serviceable, then looked at his watch: it was 21:30 hours. There was time to get some rest before embarking on the next phase of the mission. He lay back on the bed, resting his head on the lumpy pillows, haunted by his mind's action-replays of the extreme events that had led him here. At least Zane had texted him to say that Hannah had started to make slow progress on the road to recovery now. That was something.

Four hours later and Felix was waking in a cold sweat from the old, familiar dream of Day Zero. Waking to remember Dad was gone felt like a chunk had been torn from his chest, and he punched the mattress angrily. He hadn't had the nightmare since he'd passed Minos selection and he'd hoped they'd gone for good.

He thought of Sommers and Hannah, lying in their own blood. *Waking or sleeping, guess there's always going to be nightmares.*

Felix washed and brushed his teeth with bottled water, knowing this might be his last chance for a while. Within the hour, he and Chuck were back on the road, climbing up through the moonlit, snow-capped mountains.

The road swept southwards towards Hakkari. In time, Felix knew, they would drive through the towns of Sirnak, Cizre and Silopi. At that point – around five kilometres from the border – while Chuck looked for his hoodwinked imaginary groom-to-be, Felix would de-bus and sneak across the mountains and into northern Iraq on foot.

He thought of his real dad, and felt loneliness ache inside him. God, how he wanted him back.

Oh, Dad, if you could see me now. You'd tell me to stop being a bloody idiot and to get the hell out of here. Or would you be proud?

Chuck stopped the Jeep briefly to refuel with cheap, Iraqi-smuggled petrol, poured from an ancient-looking billy-can. They had to pass through scores of military checkpoints during the course of the journey, sometimes manned by soldiers, other times by Jesh – bands of AK47-wielding, baggy-trousered militiamen employed by the Turkish military to root out PKK guerrillas and persuade fellow villagers not to harbour 'undesirables'. Felix was scared someone would decide to search the car and discover his pack concealed in the boot. But the story Chuck told of the idiot groom in the truck bound for Iraq – with plenty of obscene hand gestures – seemed to amuse the guards and they were never detained for too long. Though Felix's false passport became well-thumbed, they made good progress as they climbed through the mountainous countryside. Still exhausted, Felix drifted into fitful sleep, trying to conserve his energy for the ordeal ahead.

Felix woke again in daylight and gazed out through the Jeep's grubby windows. The sandy-bronze backdrop of snow-capped mountains contrasted against the tawny grass, backed by fields of cotton, orchards and vineyards. As Chuck drove down into the town of Sirnak, fishermen cast their rods into the Tigris from its palm-fringed banks, and a call to prayer rang out from the tower of a nearby mosque.

They continued south, speeding along the highway towards Silopi. As they neared it, Felix saw hundreds of petrol tankers and cargo trucks parked up at the side of the road, presumably queuing to cross the border. He had never seen so many petrol tankers in one place before. Even with the windows up, the stink of diesel, dust, sweat and human waste almost overwhelmed him. All he wanted to do was gag.

'Not so pretty,' Chuck noted as they pulled up on the southern edge of Silopi. 'Here. Take a closer look.'

He passed across a set of battered binoculars. Felix took them and stared out over a lush, green plain. Every kilometre a Turkish army watchtower stood at the side of the road with an armed bunker dug in beside it. A short distance inside the border, roadside teashops were set up at Habur Gate, where the trucks were queuing to cross the border. Even without the bins, Felix couldn't miss the six-metre-high Kurdish flag flapping in the wind. Beside it, a border sign read WELCOME TO IRAQI KURDISTAN REGION, the intricate Arabic letters above the English like a line of fancy yellow carriages viewed side-on. The country's snow-covered mountains loomed larger now, like an oppressive, impassable wall.

Felix took a deep breath. 'This is where I get off.'

Chuck took off his shades and smiled at him. 'Good luck, son,' he said simply. Something in his eyes said he didn't think much of Felix's chances, but at least he'd decided against patronizing him with any kind of pep talk. He settled for shaking Felix firmly by the hand. 'Just mind out for the five thousand pairs of PKK eyes watching you in the mountains.'

Felix smiled ruefully. 'Will do.' He opened the car door and steeled himself for a moment in the gathering heat of the morning sunlight. 'Have a good journey yourself.'

Without further fuss, he took his pack and made his way swiftly across the mountain plateau and into the lawless foothills of the Turkish–Iraqi border.

... ELEVEN ...

Felix ran in the suffocating heat of the desert sun, sweat pouring off him, into his eyes and down his reddened face. He had reached the cover of hilly terrain, but knew that his passage across the plateau could well have been followed by guerrillas in the mountains.

After ten minutes more running, he found a depression in the ground and crouched down, panting for breath. *If I'm going to be ambushed*, he reasoned, *the most likely time is right now as they move out to intercept me.* He removed the assault rifle from his pack and placed a magazine on it, before switching the selector to safe and pulling the cocking handle to the rear.

Half an hour passed. Slowly Felix rose from out of the lying-up point and scanned the entire area with his rifle scope. It felt like he was the only person in the world. Trepidation buzzed in his guts at the prospect of the sixty-five-kilometre trek ahead of him, through the mountains to Dahuk and his waiting transport. It would be the ultimate secret arrival into Iraq.

'I can do this,' he told himself. 'It's what I signed up for. Just like running up Pen-y-Fan in mid-Wales. Only in widescreen.' He peered back at the way he'd come. 'Storey Arms Mountain Rescue Centre would be that way, while over in *this* direction we find . . . ?'

Felix set off to find out.

Soon he had reached a fast but comfortable pace. As he weaved his way through the snow-capped mountains, he felt a sense of solitude overwhelm him. Part of him felt at peace, while another part of him felt completely vulnerable; he was an outsider, an alien, alone. This was one of the most breathtaking and most dangerous regions on earth.

He stomped up through the mountain paths, thirst sucking at his throat. But he knew that until he reached Dahuk he had to stay on 'hard routine' – no hot food or drinks, as even the smell of a cup of coffee could compromise him in this clear mountain air. He'd packed plastic bags too, for crapping in; the smell of fresh human faeces was even more of a giveaway.

To slake his thirst, Felix detoured to break the ice of a nearby stream. He dropped down on one knee to take a gulp of the freezing water flowing beneath it. He felt suddenly, wildly, brilliantly alive, and wanted to whoop at the top of his lungs. *Yeah*, he reflected, *and wind up wildly, brilliantly dead*. The PKK guerrillas weren't about to welcome western strangers snooping through their territory. He pressed on through the inhospitable mountain passes, eating Brazil nuts. They were the perfect food-fit for this situation – odourless, weighed little, and were a rich source of energy and protein. *Even so*, he thought, *I'd kill for a burger*.

On Felix ran, up onto the ridgeline. The unforgiving snowfields picked up the early morning light, casting a thousand different shades of colour across the faces of the narrow hills. He stopped for a few seconds to appreciate its beauty, and swayed suddenly. He was feeling nauseous, and his head was starting to pound.

Now is not the time to pack up on me, body, Felix thought anxiously. He took out his GPS and swore as he realized he'd covered ten miles and climbed over two thousand metres in less than three hours. His instructors had warned him that on high-altitude missions he should aim for no more than three to five hundred metres of ascent for each day's climb. Nerves and adrenaline had made him push himself too hard.

He had to be experiencing the onset of acute mountain sickness. Major Fawcett had warned about that little charmer. He knew that if he didn't get to lower ground soon his nausea would turn to vomiting, his balance and co-ordination would begin to fail, he'd start coughing up bloody phlegm and then . . .

No way, Felix resolved, looking all about him. *Bad attitude is one thing, but I haven't come this far to be stopped by having the wrong* altitude . . .

He needed to descend, and quickly. His head was filled now with a blinding pain, like grenades going off in his brain. He noticed a river snaking along the valley floor. If he dropped down to meet it, he'd be able to follow its course south towards Dahuk, and the AMS would clear. Perfect solution . . . Except he knew too that any river was a magnet for shepherds in this difficult region – and any shepherd would have to be treated as a potential enemy.

So many exciting ways to die. He set off, again at a run, trying to pick the fastest path downwards while avoiding anything that would call for jumps or leaps best left to superheroes. His vision was blurring, the stark surroundings swimming in and out of focus. It was getting harder to judge distance, but he knew he had to keep heading down. The blood was roaring in his ears and his sweat was thick with the sunblock on his skin, stinging his eyes and dripping into his gaping mouth.

He checked the GPS but it was no good, the screen wouldn't hold still long enough; he would have to make do with handrailing the river, keeping it in constant sight. Bile rose in the back of his throat but he swallowed it back, stumbling onwards down the hilly tracks, willing himself to keep going: *Each step is a step closer to this headache easing off.* He thought of Hannah, still fighting in hospital. *If she can hold it together, so can you.*

Body racked with pain, eyes so sore he could barely keep them open, Felix finally collapsed behind a boulder on a ledge overlooking the river. The chill grey ribbon looked a lot brighter and wider from here. Still unable to focus on the GPS, he had to settle for praying he'd dropped far enough and that no one had seen him. The amount of noise he'd made must have carried for miles.

Felix suddenly felt horribly exposed. And he was starting to shiver. Rummaging through his pack, he pulled out an insulated foil blanket, like the kind they gave marathon runners but black on one side; he had to conserve body heat, but at least he wouldn't draw attention to himself by reflecting sunlight in all directions. Once he'd wrapped himself up, he pulled out his assault rifle and cradled it, forcing himself to breathe deeply and rest his eyes. He reacted to the tiniest sound, fearing guerrillas or soldiers or animals approaching. But slowly his symptoms began to ease. He scanned the landscape. There was still no one in sight, but he couldn't dodge the feeling that enemy eyes had clocked him.

'Seeing as I'm in no state to carry on for a bit,' Felix muttered, 'I might as well call home.' He pulled out his satphone and flicked out the aerial. A talk to the Girl might distract him from the state he was in . . .

But it was a male voice he heard – another tera-head. 'State your name and passcode.'

Felix did so quietly with a pang of disappointment. *She's got to sleep sometime*, he told himself.

'How are you feeling, Felix?' the man went on. 'We've been tracking you – you've made good time.'

'I only wish I was having one,' Felix murmured, pulling at his sweaty shirt.

'We actually need you to double back a short distance,' the tera-head went on casually.

Felix could have groaned out loud. OK, fair enough, they could hardly have called to say 'cool your heels' – if his phone went off while he was hiding from nearby guerrillas it would not be cool – but the idea of having to retrace his steps when he felt so rough . . .

The tera-head must've mistaken his weary silence for rapt attention. 'A fuller study has now been made of the extracts salvaged from the DVDs you acquired,' he went on. 'One sequence dated eight months ago shows a piece of heavy machinery being manoeuvred through terrain we've matched by satellite analysis – the area is a few miles outside Dahuk.' He read out a set of co-ordinates which Felix confirmed and programmed into his satnav. 'We don't know what relevance it has, so we need you to study the wreckage and report back.'

'I'm not exactly an engineer.'

'You're our eyes and ears out there, Felix. Use the phone camera to take video footage and use the modem to upload it from Irbil.'

'Copy that,' Felix murmured.

'We'll be tracking you,' the man said. 'Out.'

The phone went dead. The absolute hush of the mountains whispered to Felix once more, and a sudden stab of loneliness did nothing to ease the fear he felt – nor the nagging resentment that after almost killing himself to cover so much ground, he now had to work his way back.

Orders are orders, he told himself. *At least now you've got something solid to go on.*

Felix packed away his foil blanket and focused on the satnav, studying the terrain and the best route to his new destination. As he set off, his apprehension lingered like the heavy thud of his headache.

... TEN ...

The foothills south of Dahuk seemed quiet and unsullied. But as he surveyed the landscape, Felix knew hidden danger lay beneath the scrubby, rocky slopes.

Unexploded ordnance.

Landmines – a legacy of Saddam Hussein's atrocities against the Kurds of northern Iraq, suppressing their rebellion during the Iran–Iraq war. Now Saddam was long since gone but the mines remained – sleeping soldiers waiting to kill at the slightest provocation.

Felix had read up, he knew the chilling facts and figures – 8,000 victims dead since 1987 and as many again left maimed; 305 square miles of mines in Kurdistan alone, with barely a sixth of that area cleared. But it was one thing knowing the horrors of what went on, quite another to be in the thick of things.

You won't see mine on the ground, Lili had said.

What if she'd been referring not to the booby trap in her flat, but to the anti-personnel mines in this region? Through his binoculars Felix could see evidence that the land had been turned over in places. Here and there, sticks protruded upright from the grass, joining with the stumps of oak trees to mark a corridor of sorts through the wilderness.

A concealed safe track, Felix decided. *Wide enough for a large vehicle like the one in Henri's footage. And from the look of things, heading in the same direction as I am.*

He followed the trail, hoping that whoever had made it did their homework properly first, and that if the PKK were hiding out in these mountains, they had something better to do today than come after him. Here and there he found what looked like track marks frozen into the heavy soil; more evidence that a heavy vehicle had used this route. But headed where?

Felix had his answer when the path appeared to peter out before a heavily wooded area sloping sharply upwards. The satnav confirmed he'd reached the intended site. 'Bang on target,' he muttered, studying a huge pile of brushwood and vegetation ahead of him. 'And unless Henri's heavy vehicles just rusted away to nothing, there's got to be a cave behind there . . .'

There were clear signs of human habitation on the approach to the brushwood – bits of fleece, a mud-caked bottle, an old belt – and there was also a lot of scrubby undergrowth and well-worn rocks about. They screamed 'come on' at him, and needed checking out.

Around ten metres from the entrance, Felix carefully set down his pack, got down on his stomach and prepared to search for tripwires and buried pressure IEDs. He knew the smallest device was powerful enough to blow a man's leg into his stomach and blind him with the shrapnel of his own bone fragments. 'And that's not going to improve my sprinting time any,' Felix muttered.

Keeping an ear out for anything that might be coming up behind him, Felix crawled closer, his belt-buckle dragging in the dust as he scanned the ground for anything that looked out of place – the tip of a wooden stake, or a piece of fishing line . . . When discussing his missions, Dad had always banged on about looking for the absence of the normal and presence of the abnormal. Always expect the unexpected.

He pulled his tripwire-feeler from his pack and gingerly crawled forward, moving the telescopic rod parallel to the ground, but not touching it. He focused on its tip. Everything else became a blur. He raised it a few centimetres, then a few more, slowly, so slowly . . . Despite his efforts to keep an ear out for ambush, Felix realized he had become totally oblivious to all sounds around him. *What if someone's coming up behind me?* He glanced back. It was so hot. Sweat was running into his eyes, stinging them. His pulse raced as he moved the feeler left . . . slowly . . . then right . . .

No tripwires. Felix laid down the rod, started to search through the detritus with his fingertips before crawling forward half a metre and then repeating the whole process.

Finally he reached the entrance, pulled a torch from his rucksack and reached a hand tentatively towards the dry, crackling branches. Then he froze. What if his torch beam tripped a light sensor and triggered a booby trap? Plus, if there were no tripwires guarding the cave approach, then that made it all the more likely one had been rigged in the concealing material. It would take him all day to assess the threat properly and in the meantime he would be entirely exposed, a sitting target. Besides, with the brushwood pulled away it would be obvious as hell to eyes in the mountains that someone had come looking.

There's got to be another way.

Carefully he scrambled up the incline a good six metres. In all probability, any traps would be set for the unwary explorer at ground level – not for someone seeking entry to the cave from above. He carefully broke away some of the top strands of brushwood, creating a narrow slit. He hand pressed through into empty space and he dropped several sticks through into the darkness. Nothing happened, so he risked the torch, squinting down inside the cave through the small gap he'd cleared.

A silver strand of firing cable, stretched taut across the inside entrance, glimmered in the torch's glow. *So there is a tripwire.* The question this begged was obvious – *Is there a secondary waiting for anyone who gets past it?* He was too vulnerable out here to take the textbook safe approach; it was time to improvise.

Felix searched out a small boulder further up the steep slope. He manoeuvred it to the roof of the cave mouth, hurled it into the cave's blackness and then dived back against the hillside. He heard a dull clunk, held himself tensed, waiting for the blast. But nothing happened.

Heart pounding, Felix took a last check around at the hushed hillside then slung his rucksack over his shoulders, and positioned himself at the top of the cave mouth. His arm muscles bulged as he lowered himself a little way into the cool, dangerous darkness, calculating his drop, praying he wouldn't stumble into the tripwire as he landed. He felt reckless as all hell and scared to death, but a part of him was loving the rush as he let himself fall . . .

He landed in a blink, grunting as his heavy pack jarred against his back. But he kept a sure footing, listening to the rapid hiss of his breath echo back at him. The cave stank like something had crawled in and died, made him want to gag after the freshness of the air outside. But it was cool, and it was a big relief to be out of the sun's pitiless glare.

Felix turned on the torch, checking the tripwire across the hidden entrance. He shuddered. One end was attached to a steel peg hammered into a boulder, the other to a modified PMN-2 anti-personnel mine – also known as a black widow, despite its leaf-green plastic casing. It was barely the size of a DS but was packed with enough high explosive to blow both your legs off. One tug on the wire was enough to flip the striker into the stab detonator . . .

'At which point, instant makeover,' Felix murmured. 'One cave redecorated in blood and kneecap.'

Turning from the tripwire, he opened his pack. He

didn't really feel like eating, but knew he couldn't keep expending energy without putting something back – and it might just calm his still-churning stomach. He stuffed his food ration down his throat – cheese spread on brown biscuits, with a Yorkie bar to follow, eaten in the smelly darkness. Then, feeling a little more sustained, he began to explore the cave. His torchlight quickly uncovered a row of battery-powered lanterns hanging from hooks on the wall. Felix switched four of them on, and in the sickly sodium glow that spilled into the dark space he realized just what a cache he had stumbled upon.

The cavern was a kind of storehouse dominated by a huge, cylindrical machine mounted on a ten-wheeled trailer. The machine was rusted and caked with dirt. Felix had no idea what it was – part of a rocket assembly maybe? To be present in Henri's footage, it had to tie in with Orpheus somehow. What could they have wanted with it? He went all around it, taking video footage with the phone's built-in camera. The bald, circular front end was scored with deep scrapes and looked to have been partly dismantled, thick wire poking out like guts from its metal innards.

Felix moved over to a pile of wooden crates. The top one was stuffed full of automatic weapons fitted with charged magazines. M4 carbines, ideal for close-quarters combat. A bin liner on the sandy floor contained more anti-personnel mines. Six dirt bikes had been piled up against the back of the cave, stored here with their keys in the ignition. Jerry cans and cola bottles filled with petrol lay scattered around beside them. There was even an old battered Toyota Corolla parked at the back.

Shining the torch over the rear seat, Felix recoiled, staggering back through the cave as bile burned the back of his throat.

There were corpses in the car. Their skin was stretched and sallow over protruding bones, almost mummified – they had been dead some time. *That explains the smell*, he realized, steeling himself for a closer look. It was grisly, but kind of fascinating. Two of the corpses were dressed in suits, the other wore overalls sporting a logo of a red crescent behind a black tower. There was no obvious cause of death that he could see. Why had they been left here?

Felix edged round to the back of the saloon and tried to open the boot. It wasn't locked; there was nothing inside. But as he backed away to take a snap of the registration plate, his heel brushed a tarpaulin stretched over the rear wall. Cautiously he turned to examine it. With a chill, he realized it could well be the tunnel Henri had immortalized on DVD. Dark space lay behind the tarpaulin, and as he used his telescopic rod to check the edges for concealed booby traps, a hideous stench of decay caught in his nostrils. What the hell was back here?

When he ventured to pull the tarpaulin back a little way and shone his torch inside, Felix realized 'hell' was right.

It was like a mass underground grave. There were bodies and bones everywhere, piled up in heaps along with a scattering of charred and broken possessions. Stunned with horror, his stomach turning, Felix cast about with the torch beam. He estimated seventy to one hundred people. The back of the cave seemed to have collapsed, giving some of the corpses an impromptu burial. But beyond the rockfall, who knew how far the open grave extended?

The village that was razed to the ground outside Irbil, Felix remembered. Was this where the victims wound up? Or had the survivors been taken here by Orpheus to be killed?

And if so, why?

... NINE ...

Trying to hold onto the food he'd just gulped down, Felix held up the phone and torch and took a video of the bodies. It was hard to believe these warped and withered remains had once been men and women and children. But even in this state, they were a hundred times more human than the Orpheus scum who must've done this to them.

Then suddenly he heard a noise outside. An animal, come scavenging? No, whatever was approaching, its tread was too stealthy. Felix's blood ran colder than the cave air; if someone was approaching with caution it could only mean they knew he was inside.

All that crashing down the mountainside I did. Someone saw me.

Stuffing the camera into his pocket, Felix ran lightly to where his pack lay near the concealed entrance of the cave. Whoever was coming must know about the tripwire – unless they were PKK agents, not Orpheus, and had simply tracked him here to take him for questioning – or to have him shot. He slung the pack on his back, switched off the lanterns on the wall and crept back to the tarpaulin at the rear of the cave. He swung the torch beam this way and that over the fallen rocks at the back of the underground grave, looking for a way through. But there was nothing. He considered concealing himself among the bodies but if he'd been seen coming in, hiding would do no good – his own corpse would be added to the pile soon enough.

The thick pile of brushwood rustled and chattered, left and right. At least two people were outside, pulling it away. With a heart thumping in time with his headache, Felix made to pull out his assault rifle. With the element of surprise he could take out whoever was first to enter the cave before the lead started flying back at him. But then he hesitated; who knew how many more aggressors might be swarming outside? If a shot hit one of the PMN-2s he'd be blasted to hell and his evidence with him. And it was the evidence that was important here – getting the footage back to Minos so they could make some sense of what he'd found, and use the knowledge to stop Orpheus. He couldn't send a thing from in here – the Thuraya's aerial needed uninterrupted access to a satellite in order to properly connect, a clear shot at the sky. He *had* to get out.

Suddenly a harsh male voice shouted out in a language Felix couldn't comprehend – Arabic or Kurdish, he wasn't sure, but each syllable exploded into the cave like shrapnel. A warning? A threat? A short burst of gunfire followed it into the cave, and Felix dived behind the huge metal carcass of the gutted rocket on its trailer. Bullets ricocheted through the darkness.

So much for the element of surprise, thought Felix. And yet, no more shots followed – only a low murmur of conversation. Perhaps the men didn't know for sure he was in here. But they would find out. He turned to the dirt bikes, stashed here presumably for crossing between camps in the foothills. Perhaps he could surprise his enemies yet . . .

The men went on clawing away the brushwood, concentrating on an area in the middle around waist height, which suggested they *did* know about the tripwire. Were they Orpheus lackeys or did they figure higher in the command structure? There was no way to tell, but at least the scraping, crunching noise covered Felix's movements as he pulled the nearest of the dirt bikes from the wall and swung a leg across the saddle. It was a two-stroke, an old dirty grey Yamaha DT125 with a cracked windshield. His dad used to drive one like it. Felix had taken it out when he was ten and crashed the thing; Dad had come down on him like a ton of . . .

Felix pushed away the memories as he wheeled the bike to the back of the cave, reached beneath the seat to turn on the fuel tap. Daylight was showing through the cave mouth, the men were shouting again – at him, or at each other, he couldn't tell. Gritting his teeth, he kick-started the bike. The choking splutter of the engine sounded loud as a bomb blast, and was answered by the rattle of gunfire and a hail of bullets from outside. Rock chips and flecks of dust peppered the air. Felix twisted hard on the throttle, felt the vibration shake through his body as the bike roared in readiness.

As the gunfire ceased and the angry voices got louder, Felix pulled the clutch and revved the throttle at the same time, shifted into first and moved forward slowly. *If you're gonna go, take the enemy with you*, he thought grimly as he leaned back on the bike and accelerated hard, pulling a wheelie as he tore across the sandy floor. Through the thin curtain of brushwood remaining he glimpsed two men dive aside as the front wheel crashed through the barrier and the back wheel rolled over the tripwire.

The noise of the explosion hit Felix's ears like hammers, and he felt the heat of the blast singe his hair. The cave spewed rock, dust and smoke after him in a violent rush, and the two men were lost from sight in the storm. Felix let the front wheel drop down with a thump, changed up into third gear, unable to believe he was still alive as he sped away. He wanted to laugh and cheer – but then, as he skidded round the next corner, he saw a pick-up truck parked sideways across the track about 300 metres ahead, blocking the way. Two men were crouched in the back with more automatics, their faces fixed in hatred. They opened fire and Felix swung sharply from the track. Getting out of range was his only chance.

But that meant driving like a maniac straight into Saddam's old minefield.

Swearing at the top of his lungs, Felix clung to the

bike and waited for the inevitable. He knew that the Iraqi soldiers back then had a Russian-style training, and so had laid their minefields in fairly set patterns – but the only way he'd know for sure what that pattern was, was when he struck one. Even if he drove through a trip flare it was doubtful he could stop before running over the double row of fragmentation mines that would most likely lie beyond it. He had to get back to the safe path.

Then, glancing behind him, he saw another dirt bike tracking him, its rider wielding an assault rifle in one hand as he bumped expertly over the uneven terrain. Of course, the man could follow Felix's path and know it was safe – in the same way soldiers used to drive sheep across minefields. He fired, and Felix felt his rucksack jump and dip on his back as bullets slammed into it. Luckily his kit was blocking the bullets – so far. He accelerated, heart in his mouth as he hurtled down a steep hillside, steering wildly around rocks and bushes and tree stumps.

Then he saw a rocky ledge protruding from the hillside to his left and, in desperation, swung the bike towards it. It was a crazy, stupid jump; with luck his pursuer would bottle it. *With even more luck*, thought Felix, *I might survive it myself*.

A lurch went through Felix's body as his bike launched into the air and seemed to fly for a long, breathless moment – but as his front wheel rammed the ground, the heavy pack on his back finally over-balanced him. With a helpless shout, Felix was thrown to the ground, his rucksack breaking his fall as he skidded and tumbled through dirt. A few seconds later his pursuer took the jump too and flew through the air, gun raised and ready – only to careen into Felix's fallen bike. The impact threw the driver clear, but his bike somersaulted onwards down the rocky slope – and then exploded in a colossal fireball that blew the bike's fuel tank apart in a secondary blast. Felix rolled over as shrapnel daggered his rucksack – then froze, palms flat in the dust. His face was centimetres from another tripwire.

Panting for breath, sick from exertion and sweating like a madman, Felix turned to find his assailant's scorched body had been staked through the chest with the front axle of his shattered dirt bike. 'Oh my God,' he whispered, feeling bile rising up in his throat as he sat back down heavily. 'That was so nearly me.'

He stared at the body for a full minute, feeling frozen inside. Then, finally, he got up and slipped the pack from his bruised and blistered shoulders. It was shot full of holes. A cursory inspection showed that it was his high-speed data transfer device that had stopped several slugs from tearing through his back; it was clearly knackered. Worse still, he'd snapped his phone's aerial in the fall. He couldn't even get in touch with Minos, let alone upload his footage, until he found somewhere with a good internet connection.

'At least *I'm* still intact,' Felix muttered, eyeing the flaming, twisted wreckage of the two dirt bikes. 'Probably.' Black smoke was belching into the air; it would draw the terrorists' Orpheus friends here like a magnet.

He turned and stared eastwards down the slope. Unless he was mistaken, the wide, snaking safe-track was bending into the brush a few hundred metres away. If he could only cross the terrain between here and there . . .

Do it, he told himself, *before the boys in that pick-up come looking*.

He drained the last of his water ration and lifted the pack back onto his shoulders. Carefully, but as quickly as he dared, Felix headed for the dubious safety of the pathway and the hilly terrain beyond it, once again on the track to Dahuk.

... EIGHT ...

Night fell, but the perfect crescent moon hovered cannily in the sky over the outskirts of Dahuk. Footsore, exhausted and more than a little paranoid, Felix strode doggedly past broken streetlamps, three-storey white-washed houses with flat roofs and blocks of muddy stone huts. Thank God for the GPS, and those clever little satellites twinkling high above; they'd guided him here unerringly. He'd been keeping to the shadows and dark, scrubby undergrowth so far, but now he'd reached a true urban area. He knew thousands of Kurds lived in this maze of darkened, stinking streets, but the town seemed eerily calm.

Then the thrum of a car engine sounded distantly behind him. He turned in time to find the twin glare of headlamps upon him. With a screech of tyres, a Merc sped forward towards him. Felix's hand strayed to the

SIG in his hip holster; he pulled it out, ready to fire . . .

'No! Please, no!' The man behind the wheel leaned his head out of the window as he screeched to a halt. 'I am a friend. Abdul-Rahim!' He jumped out of the car and his toothy grin caught the moonlight. He wore loose-fitting trousers, a dark tunic with an embroidered neck and a crumpled thigh-length jacket. 'Here to take you onwards.'

'How did you know where to find me?' Felix demanded.

'I got a call. ATLAS have your tracker, right? But you haven't called in and they couldn't contact you. So they sent me to the area.'

'The phone's bust,' Felix said.

'Ah. I've been driving round Dahuk searching for you. *Combing* the area, you say?'

Felix nodded wearily. 'Please, can I get in?'

'Of course.' Abdul-Rahim opened the rear passenger door.

'Thanks.' Felix threw his pack on the back seat and eased himself in after it.

Abdul-Rahim watched him with sympathy. 'A difficult journey?'

'You couldn't make it up, mate.' Felix closed his eyes and revelled in the luxury of the soft, cracked seat leather, and no weight on his feet. Despite his exhaustion, as the car pulled away he felt a quiet thrill of pride. He'd made the crossing. He'd survived. And now someone was here to look after him, to take him the rest of the distance.

He was so grateful to Abdul-Rahim he could've cried. Instead, he fell almost instantly into a dreamless sleep.

The road to Dahuk from Irbil was long, dusty and uncomfortable. Felix's sleep had been broken by the pot-holes and craters in the tarmac, and the car's suspension would surely soon follow. It didn't help that Abdul-Rahim drove the taxi like he was racing some invisible opponent.

'So, you'll know from your walk that it's a beautiful country, right?' Abdul-Rahim smiled at him in the rear-view mirror, taking his eyes off the road for rather longer than Felix would have liked. 'And you're enjoying the ride now?'

'The ride's great, Abdul-Rahim,' Felix assured him.

'Abdul, please.'

'And it's the most beautiful place I've ever seen. Uh, not that I've been abroad much.'

'You are still young,' Abdul declared. 'So much time ahead.'

Felix stared out of the window at the incredible mountainous vista all around him. It made him feel so small. 'Here's hoping.'

'As you say, Junior.' Abdul grinned into the rear-view. 'Here's hoping for a full life. And, of course, full pockets.'

Felix smiled too, but more to himself than to the driver. Chuck had already told him plenty about Abdul-Rahim — a former conscript from Istanbul and one of ATLAS's conscious contacts: a civilian called upon from time to time to give his services in the fight against global terrorism. *He knows not to ask too many questions,*

Chuck had assured him. *He'll probably ask for money instead.*

Nevertheless, Felix found that he trusted Abdul from the moment he'd met him. And besides, just to be able to sit down and let someone else worry about movement and direction felt a real luxury.

He watched as they passed eighteen-wheelers grinding slowly up the steep foothills, bulging with bags of cement and scaffolding.

'Abdul, have you been told anything about this mission?' Felix wondered.

'Nothing, Junior, and I prefer it that way.' Abdul smiled again. 'I'm here to make your job easier. But please keep the details to yourself, always.'

'Right now I don't *have* many details,' Felix admitted. 'I need somewhere with secure Wi-Fi access. And a giant-sized breakfast.'

'My cousin can provide this. He runs an internet café; it's where ATLAS contact me.' He clapped Felix on the shoulder. 'And as you're with me, my cousin may even give you a discount.'

Felix's Seamaster was ticking off a third hour by the time they reached Irbil. The sun was shining brightly overhead and the day was still young and warm. Abdul's Merc rattled through the sprawling mass of flat-faced, sand-coloured homes and chunky-looking concrete apartment blocks. Planes scraped a white trail across the blue sky, rising up from the newly extended airport.

Soon they had reached the busy centre of town,

where modern architecture clashed with old stone in tall urban canyons. Some of the streets were drab concrete affairs with tangles of electrical wires hanging down almost to the pavement. Others were as thronged with signs and advertising hoardings as they were with people, fifty things at once vying for Felix's attention as the car stopped and started through the traffic. It was scarcely better in the old part of the city, where an ancient sandstone citadel rose up like a weather-worn coronet from a wide, scrubby hill. A tight mass of shops and market stalls crammed up against the road, huddled together as if for comfort, their tin roofs sagging. Awnings made from blankets and tarpaulins flapped from scaffolding poles in the dry breeze like unofficial flags.

Abdul stopped the car outside a fast-food café. The smell of spices and frying meat mingled with the reek of diesel generators and excrement. Felix stretched stiffly as he got out of the car with his pack. The market place seemed a kaleidoscope of colour, noise and chaos, and he was surprised to find that many people looked European.

'Northern Iraq has always been a crossroads between Europe and Asia,' Abdul explained. 'Makes it fun for the hotel police. They keep tabs on everyone coming in and out. Not easy . . .'

'Which suits me,' said Felix. 'But also suits Orpheus.'

Abdul ushered him through a sheet of thick tarp into a surprisingly modern office space with imitation wood floors and snug little booths. Felix hung back as Abdul greeted a man in a linen suit with kisses to the cheeks, and a minute or so later he was led to a small tobacco-stinking office at the back where a rattling air con unit was losing its battle against the stifling heat. The man, Abdul's cousin presumably, logged him onto his own PC with a dual Arabic-English keyboard.

Once the man had retired, Felix connected his mobile. The connection was supposed to be high-speed, but uploading the pictures from the camera to his phone browser was taking roughly for ever. At least it gave him time to rig a temporary repair to the phone aerial.

Abdul came into the room after half an hour or so with a tray loaded with round bread, a variety of cheeses, carrot jam and a thick white sauce that might have been hummus. Felix tucked in hungrily, savouring every bite.

'Hey,' said Abdul suddenly, looking at the picture of the Toyota on the camera's viewscreen. 'That car . . .'

Felix's heart leaped. 'You recognize it?'

'Oh, yes indeed.' Abdul nodded. 'I always wanted a car like that.'

'Thanks for your input,' Felix muttered through a mouthful of bread and jam.

'Ah, and *that* I recognize too,' Abdul went on, pointing to the logo on the dead man's overalls that Felix had filmed close-up.

'I know, I know – a moon and a rectangle, right?'

'Seriously,' insisted Abdul. 'It is an international firm based in Irbil – Blackmoon Construction. Big firm, lots of contract work here and in Iran, and Europe—'

Felix nearly spat out his chunk of bread. 'Can you take me there?'

'Of course,' Abdul said amiably. 'I have a cousin in the

building trade; he has worked for Blackmoon. I know where it is and we can go there . . .' He smiled sheepishly. 'For a small consideration?'

'I think we can deal,' Felix told him, pulling a wad of notes from his pocket and counting off 200,000 dinar – about a hundred pounds.

Abdul took the notes and counted them with an apologetic look. 'It pains me I must do this – but it is ten thousand more for the delicious food you are eating.'

'Worth every penny,' said Felix, peeling off another bill. 'And while we're playing, do you recognize this?' He brought up the picture of the trailer-mounted cylinder-thing he'd found in the cave.

'It seems familiar . . .' Felix impatiently offered him still more money, but Abdul shook his head. 'If I remember, you can share my memory for free . . .' He started nodding, faster and faster. 'Yes, of course. I've seen such machines in Turkey – tunnel-boring machines.'

'Tunnel-boring?'

'Sure, like digging out sewage tunnels, or tunnels for railways—'

'Or tunnels between borders,' Felix realized, almost wincing at how hard the penny dropped. 'Henri was from Rafah, an expert in building tunnels for smuggling between Palestine and Egypt . . . Maybe that video footage he took wasn't of caves, but of *tunnels*. The boring-machine was left there; perhaps it was used to carve out that mass grave . . .'

Abdul looked blank. 'I do not understand, my friend, nor do I wish to.'

Felix sat down at the PC, opened up a new window in the net browser and tapped 'tunnel-boring' into Google. A second later the first page of links appeared, with a handful of images at the top, and straight away he saw how the gutted hulk in the cave must once have looked when in service. '*Double-shielded, earth pressure balance tunnel-boring,*' he read aloud; it might as well have been Shakespeare for all the sense it made. Felix tried another link. '*The tunnel can be driven an average of forty-two metres per day with our machines, with certain strata yielding even faster rates of progress—*' He broke off, staring at Abdul. 'Lili said something about driving and a tunnel. Must've got it from Henri – his special talent was in making tunnels for smugglers under the Gaza Strip. Kanska maybe used him to build a tunnel someplace . . .'

'Who are these people? I don't want to know.'

'Driving must be the engineers' word for boring through the rock.'

Abdul yawned. 'Tunnel-boring. That's well named.'

'If Lili was using her last words to talk about it, it *has* to be important,' Felix muttered, balling his fists in frustration. 'If only we had more of Henri's evidence to go on. Orpheus are planning some massive atrocity but we still know jack all about where and when it's meant to be taking place . . .'

'This picture you've taken shows the machine stripped down to a shell,' Abdul said thoughtfully. 'Why should that be?'

'Maybe when they finished whatever tunnels they were building, the thing broke down and they sold on the parts.'

'Orpheus trading in spare? It does not sound likely.' Abdul shook his head. 'And I cannot see them buying up old machines of this size and restoring them for sale at a profit. Not their style. Besides, they are such specialist machines, there cannot be many, so stolen ones that were sold on would be easy to trace.'

Felix nodded ruefully. 'Maybe they only realized that once they'd bought a whole load of tunnel-borers,' he joked, 'and they've had to hide a job lot in caves around here . . .'

'Wait a moment.' Abdul looked at him. 'What if they do have more of these machines, Junior? They are driving their tunnels somewhere else – in a whole other country maybe – and they only stole *this* one for spares to keep their small fleet running!'

'Abdul, you're brilliant.' Felix leaped up from his chair in excitement. 'And if Blackmoon Construction are an international outfit, they could have transported those parts.' He stuffed some more food into his mouth as the connections kept sparking through his mind. He remembered the scrap of 'incriminating' footage that showed Rashed being led out of the truck . . . and how Rashed's body had wound up riddled with radiation. 'Maybe Kanska has been transporting people as well as machine spares to keep the tunnel-borers drilling. He could have smuggled Rashed into the UK, along with radioactive stuff. Maybe he's building *dirty* bombs?'

Abdul put his fingers in his ears. 'I think I'm hearing too much, now.'

Felix shook his head, pulled Abdul's hands away. 'We

need to find records of what Blackmoon have been shipping where. We need to pay these people a visit, right now.'

'Very well, Junior. Your taxi awaits.' Abdul rose and clapped him on the back. 'But first, did you enjoy your meal?'

'It was spot-on. Thanks.'

Abdul held out his hand and waited. 'And do you not tip for good service, my friend?'

...SEVEN...

Felix and Abdul were back out into the colour and fuss of the Old City within ten minutes, setting off the moment the video footage had been uploaded to ATLAS's file transfer site for full analysis. Felix had tested his phone by calling in to the tera-heads. It was the man who took his call. He seemed genuinely relieved that contact had been re-established and praised the fresh evidence and discovery of the possible connection to Blackmoon, but the only information he would pass on concerning Hannah was that her condition was stable. Disappointed, Felix announced he was looking more closely into Blackmoon and said he'd call in within six hours or when-ever he had more information.

His thoughts lingered with unease on the shrunken corpses in the Toyota, and what chain of events had led them to be dumped in the back of a car beside an improvised graveyard in the middle of nowhere. Maybe they were legit and had wanted no part in the village massacre – or in whatever else Orpheus was up to, just like Lili and Henri in the end . . .

Felix didn't kid himself that he was a Brain of Britain, but he hated not having the answers. What Minos needed was hard proof, not guesswork.

And that was what he intended to get, whatever it took.

They drove on through the thronging streets, out of the Old Town and passing the new developments, into more open countryside. Felix stared out at the sweeps of sand stretching far into the distance and the vast brooding presence of the mountains, as the roads became dustier and in poor repair.

Then, etched onto the side of a huge brown industrial cube of a building, Felix saw the Blackmoon logo, and felt a shiver quake through him.

Abdul pulled into the car park, which was little more than a flat rectangle of mud bordering scrubby grazing land and desert. A dead dog lay by the roadside, its body clouded by flies. There weren't many cars about – but then, it was a Saturday.

'What's your plan?' Abdul wondered as he stopped the car. 'Well, show your bosses you're the big man, sure – but how?'

Felix chewed his lip. 'For a start I can try cloning Blackmoon's computers' hard drives and take the data back to your cousin's net café for sending back to ATLAS so their experts can translate it.'

'And how will you do this cloning?'

'By downloading a utility file from the net,' Felix told him. 'But first, I need a big enough distraction to get me access to their computers. How about we set off the fire alarm?'

'This is a war zone. You think we care about fire alarms?' Abdul pulled a pitta bulging with salad from a plastic lunchbox on the passenger seat and shook his head. 'If we don't smell smoke we don't fear the flames.'

Felix considered. 'So let's start a fire.'

'A fire,' Abdul grumbled through a mouthful of lettuce. 'We could get arrested!'

'If we're lucky,' Felix agreed, rummaging in his pack for his wet-and-windies – military-issue matches that lit well in all conditions. He tossed the little box to Abdul. 'Use this, find a nice quiet spot away from anywhere and get fire-starting.'

'You are trying to make me the big man too, huh?' Abdul didn't look happy. 'And the bigger target.'

'Big man equals big bucks,' Felix encouraged him. 'While you do that, I'll blag my way to reception and try to find out where their computers are kept.'

Abdul put the matches in his lunchbox and hid them beneath the half-eaten pitta. 'There. Now if I'm questioned, none will suspect my true motives.'

'They'll suspect you've got a weird appetite.' Felix smiled. 'It's the weekend, it should be pretty quiet. Just act like you own the place. If people see you look confident, they'll probably leave you alone.'

'You learned this in training?'

'Yeah. Nice of you to try it out and see if it actually works.' Felix ran a sweaty hand through his hair and pulled on his backpack, wincing as it scraped his cuts and bruises. 'If I don't see you sooner, rendezvous back here in forty minutes.'

'At eighteen hundred hours.' Abdul checked his watch, nodded and touched his heart. 'Good luck. And mind out for security cameras!'

Felix left the car and headed for the company's reception block, sweating in the warm evening air. Inside, a young, clean-shaven man was sitting behind a desk in a reclining chair, speaking loudly on the phone in Arabic. Felix slipped off his pack and gave him a hopeful smile, which had little visible effect. Six TV monitors were stacked on a table behind the man, showing different views of the building yard. Hopefully that meant there was no dedicated security team with their own station on site – just this not-very-diligent receptionist.

Abdul strode into view on one of the security monitors, beetling towards a storehouse in one corner of the yard. Felix willed the receptionist not to turn round – and it worked. A little too well, maybe; it wasn't for about another two minutes that the man finally wound up his phone conversation and looked up at Felix.

'American?' said the receptionist simply.

'British,' Felix told him, grateful that the man spoke his language at all. 'My father's been installing a new computer system here. I'm supposed to meet him here in the . . . IT department? Data centre?'

The man considered, shook his head. 'No one comes here today.'

'Are you sure?'

The visitors' book, empty of entries, was pushed over the desk towards him. Felix made a great show of looking puzzled. 'I don't understand . . . I thought I saw him out there in the car park, walking out of that old building at the front.'

The man shook his head. 'You can't have. Our computers are in the new building, round the back.'

Thanks very much for the info, thought Felix, carefully keeping his puzzled frown in place. 'Oh. I'm sorry, I must have the wrong company. Thanks for your help.'

With a brief smile and a nod, the man reached for his phone again and dialled. *That's right*, he thought, shuffling out of reception. *Forget about me. Please.*

Once outside, Felix gazed about, searching for the security cameras on their long white poles, trying to work out which one had picked up Abdul and where he might be now. Then, as luck would have it, he spied his driver walking back towards him, a stolen hod clutched in both hands, empty save for a few red clay bricks – and one plastic lunchbox.

Felix hurried up to Abdul. 'Job done,' the man said quietly. 'There's much timber stored here. And much petrol. The effect of putting them together with a lit match should be noticed quite soon.'

'I'm not sure who by. The place looks pretty deserted.' Felix looked at him. 'Did anyone see you?'

'Only a camel spider.' Abdul picked up his lunchbox. 'He won't talk. I put him in here.'

Felix saw a huge, shadowy blur inside the box and shivered slightly. 'Why, for God's sake?'

'My cousin, he collects rare spiders and snakes. Will pay!'

'It figures.' Felix peered about. Nothing stirred. 'Come on. Let's scout around the back.'

'I'm supposed to be just your taxi driver.'

'Please. I can't read the signs here. And I'll pay extra.'

'Well . . .' Abdul wavered. 'I suppose I cannot leave a friend in need.'

'Not if he's got his wallet,' agreed Felix. 'You've got the hod. Pretend you're escorting me or something.'

The two of them walked through the muddy yard. Scaffolding lay rusting in unkempt piles, and a huge generator the size of a tank buzzed and rumbled in a corrugated iron shack that had seen better days. Cables snaked from it to a new red plastic industrial unit in the far corner of the muddy yard. '*Records Office*,' Abdul read the sign above the door aloud. 'Could that be what you're after?'

'Got to be worth a try,' Felix agreed. He and Abdul walked to the far side of the building and then ducked down as they reached an open window. Felix peered carefully inside.

'No one home,' he observed, as distant shouts carried from the far part of the building yard. 'But it sounds like someone's around, anyway. And hopefully your little blaze will keep them from wandering back here for a few minutes.'

'Be fast, Junior,' Abdul told him. 'I feel we are pushing our luck.' He put down the hod and picked up the lunch-box. 'Now my work is done, I shall wait for you in the car. And I shall keep the engine running.'

'Do that.' Felix checked no one was around, and then eased open the window, pushed his pack inside and quickly climbed in after it. The records office boasted two battered old PCs and a smart-looking laptop, all of them up and running, and sharing a network – a wireless router sat beneath one of the desks, its array of green lights watching him like little eyes.

Pulling a portable hard disk from his jacket pocket, Felix firewired it to the laptop and started downloading the disk copy utility that would allow him to back up all information on the network. By cloning the raw data on the drives, he could even take away the digital remains of deleted files for close analysis, increasing their chances of learning where in the world any *special* consignments had been sent . . .

But then suddenly, a man in a sweat-stained suit burst into the room, snarling in Arabic and wielding an assault rifle. A jolt of shock slammed through Felix. He recognized the dark and hate-filled eyes in the sallow face. It was one of the men from the pick-up in the foothills.

An Orpheus agent.

... SIX ...

Holding himself very still, Felix realized there was no surprise on the newcomer's face. *The receptionist*, he realized with a sinking feeling. *The whole of Blackmoon is bent. All that chat – he must've quietly raised an alarm somehow, kept on talking to give his Orpheus bosses time to prepare. No wonder this place was such a cinch to get into.*

The man kept the rifle trained on Felix's chest as he said something in his own tongue that Felix didn't understand. *He shot and missed me once, he's not going to make that mistake again.* Felix could feel his own handgun nudging his ribs, but knew he'd never reach it. Smoke and the reek of petrol blew in through the open window, and he wondered if he stood a chance of leaping out before the man could fire. Reason screamed *No way*, but desperation was shouting louder and he tensed himself ready to jump . . .

Suddenly the man's mobile phone rang out. He looked down automatically to answer it.

And Felix took his chance.

He vaulted the desk, away from the window. The terrorist looked up, raised his gun – but Felix kicked it away, following up with a right hook to the jaw that nearly broke his knuckles. The man shouted out, smashed into the doorframe – and went down.

Felix scooped up the fallen assault rifle and drew his own handgun. Keeping the man covered, he cautiously looked out through the inner doorway for any other surprises. But the offices seemed empty. Felix supposed that if there were anyone nearby, they wouldn't have needed to call.

The hapless gunman groaned as he came round. Alerted by the sound, Felix went back into the room – just as Abdul's head popped up into view at the window.

'You OK, Junior?' he hissed. 'I heard a shout.'

'And you came back? Thanks. Now, get in here, can you? Before you're spotted.' Abdul clambered in, and Felix passed him the assault rifle before turning back to the computer screen. 'Keep this guy covered while I finish up here.'

The man opened his eyes, and at once looked both fearful and outraged. Abdul held the gun with wary disdain.

'What has this company been smuggling – other than Fenar Rashed into the UK?' The terrorist didn't answer, but Felix saw him react at the name. 'So that *is* how he got into Britain.' He looked anxiously at his portable hard drive, still storing all that gathered digital info, and prayed the much-needed info would be here and recoverable. Then he looked back at the man on the floor. 'What's your name?'

Again, silence. Abdul encouraged him in his own language, noisily slipping the safety off the gun. He got a muttered response: 'Predrag.'

'Abdul, tell Predrag we know Orpheus has been tunnelling, and that Kanska's been recruiting lensmen in Eastern Europe. What's going down?'

Abdul translated, but Predrag kept his teeth clenched together, his lips pursed.

'I'm sure we can piece the plot together from the info on your computer,' said Felix, deepening his voice a little and aiming his gun at Predrag's leg. 'But you'd save us a lot of time, hassle and clearing up if you'd talk,' he swallowed hard. I'd sooner this interrogation was "unenhanced" but if we have to get rough . . .'

'You are a child,' Predrag muttered in English.

'And you're history if you don't start talking,' Felix snapped. 'I'm not playing at this. Abdul, is the coast clear?'

Abdul glanced around and nodded.

Felix gritted his teeth, aimed carefully and fired his gun, and a bullet hole appeared in the floor beside Predrag's ankle. The man moaned with fear.

'Since I'm just a kid, you won't be wanting me taking any more random shots,' said Felix. 'Right?'

Looking downcast at the floor, Predrag slowly nodded.

'So, what happened to those men you dumped in the back of the Toyota? We know one of them worked here.'

Predrag looked at Abdul and spoke in a garbled rush. Abdul interpreted. 'The men were exposed too long to a consignment of . . .' He turned to Felix, fear in his eyes. 'Plutonium. They tested a bomb beneath the outskirts of town. It went wrong. Village destroyed, they had to remove all trace. Some of the workmen got sick . . . Radiation sick. So they were brought underground through a tunnel Orpheus made and left to die. No one could bury them – couldn't risk discovery . . .'

'In case the authorities found out the corpses had radiation poisoning.' Felix stared at Predrag. 'Is that what's going on? You're making nuclear bombs here in Irbil and exporting them to other countries?'

The man nodded again and spoke in a rush, a sneer on his face and arrogance in his eyes. Felix felt a chill as he recognized words and letters – *JFK, LAX, Tokyo Narita, Manchester* . . .

Abdul whirled round to face Felix. 'He says there are bombs buried in tunnels beneath four major airports. That you can't stop him.'

Felix felt sick. He thought of Zane describing the security measures that were keeping New Heathrow secure. *While we guard the reopening of one airport with everything we've got, Orpheus strikes at four others.* He shook his head in horror. *Just four days from now.* It made a kind of perfect, callous sense; he'd read that Manchester had always been the busiest airport outside London, and in the Day Zero aftermath it had expanded to accommodate millions more passengers. 'No wonder Kanska's been after lensmen to capture the action.'

'Who would film such a thing as a nuclear blast?' Abdul hissed. 'They would die themselves.'

'To have dodged security the bombs must be down pretty deep,' Felix reckoned. 'They'll destroy the foundations and topple the airports, but at least the radioactive fallout will be contained.' He looked down at their prisoner. 'What about the diagram Rashed was carrying, showing the overwatch point? The towers or skyscrapers or whatever they are.'

The man spat, then gabbled something hoarsely. 'He says he's told us enough.'

And thanks to that, we're going to stop Orpheus. Felix felt supercharged with adrenaline. *Thanks to me.*

Abruptly, the laptop beeped, rousing him with confirmation that he had successfully cloned the network drives – though that hardly seemed to matter now. 'Keep him covered, Abdul,' said Felix. He pulled out the hard drive with trembling fingers and stuck it in the pocket of his cargo pants. 'I've got to let Minos know what's happening.'

Abdul gripped the gun, looking overwhelmed. 'You're the big man, now, for sure.'

'There's still a long way to go,' said Felix, reminding himself as well as Abdul. He pulled out the satphone, checked his repair to the aerial was holding, and ducked outside through the window to get an uninterrupted signal. As he speed-dialled Minos he felt his heart bumping hard with adrenaline. He'd done his job – a single kid sent out into the dangerous unknown had blown apart a major terrorist plot. *No more Day Zeros*, he thought fiercely. *No more kids like me, screaming on their own while their fathers burn*.

He forced himself to delay calling until he'd checked properly that the immediate area was clear. He couldn't afford to blow things now. But it seemed eerily still in the yard. He could look behind the various huts and brick-stacks to make sure they were clear, but might easily be spotted in the act. Besides, surely Abdul's fire would be keeping the workforce busy?

Warily, Felix hunkered down behind a pile of concrete slabs. Then he phoned.

'State your name and passcode.'

It was the Girl, no less. Things were getting better and better. 'Felix Smith, passcode one-one-seven-nine,' he said quickly. 'Have apprehended agent of Orpheus with assistance from conscious contact. Possible other enemies on site, but I've got intelligence I need to—'

'Where are you?'

'Can't you tell? Is my tracker not working?'

'Confirm for me, please.'

Felix frowned with irritation. 'Blackmoon Construction, southern Irbil, OK? It's me, I'm for real. Now, listen. I know what Orpheus are planning and it's timed for the opening of New Heathrow in four days' time. Nuclear devices are due to be detonated in the areas of Manchester Airport, JFK Airport in New York, Los Angeles International and Tokyo Narita . . .'

There was a tense silence. 'Nuclear?' the Girl said at last, calmly. 'You have proof?'

'Confession from one of their agents,' Felix went on breathlessly. 'Turns out the corpses I found in the cave were poisoned by radiation – just as Rashed was. They were dry-running construction and detonation of a nuclear bomb underground here in Irbil, testing their technique to explode in Britain, America and Japan.' She didn't respond, and he couldn't help feeling disappointed. 'What's up, is that not enough terror for a tera-head?'

'A confession made by an Orpheus agent under duress—'

'What about that tunnelling equipment from Henri's footage I found,' Felix said impatiently. 'It must've been stripped down for spares to be used in similar machines around the world.'

'Do you have confirmation of the diagram's purpose?' she said, still sounding unruffled. 'Only there's still no sky-line match despite a global search.'

'I think maybe it's a hoax,' said Felix, 'designed to mislead us into looking above ground when the real threat is hidden *under* the ground.'

'I'll pass this on at once,' the Girl said. 'You'll need to make a priority report to Zane as soon as he's available. What's your situation now?'

'I'm going to attempt to leave site with conscious contact and prisoner. We'll keep him tied up in Abdul's car.'

'We'll consult with ATLAS and see what transportation's available to get you back to the UK.'

Felix mentally punched the air. He couldn't wait to get back. 'What's the cover story this time?'

'I'll let you know.'

'And will you say well done?'

She paused. 'Well done.'

'You coming out to celebrate when I get back?'

'Just get back in one piece, OK?'

'Copy that. Felix out.' As he tucked away the phone a thrill of triumph surged through him – which abruptly drained away as he heard a hoarse cry from Abdul in the office, along with a heavy clatter. Next instant, with a violent shattering of glass, Abdul flew backwards through the office window and lay groaning on his back in the dust.

At the same time he saw two more men jump out from hiding behind the records office, their M16s trained on Felix's chest. Icy fear tangled through his body. He was about to reach for the pistol in his shoulder holster – but then something hard and cold pushed into his neck as someone stepped up behind him.

'One move and I take your head off,' came a wheezing hiss in Felix's ear. Then the man moved round into sight.

Oh. God.

It was Supyan Kanska. The terrorist overlord. As the snatch of video had proved, he'd aged badly since the mug shot Zane had produced; he was now completely bald, and thinner too – the skin stretched tight over his sharp, chiselled features. 'A perfect performance, Felix Smith. Thank you.' His accent made the words smoulder and curl. 'A gifted child for sure. But still a child. Like the girl Rashed observed keeping watch on poor, doomed Lili.' He smiled. 'Are resources so low that this is the best GI5 can send against Orpheus? It is insulting. They must be more desperate than I had believed.'

Felix was disgusted with himself. He'd been so eager to call in his revelations, his check on the yard had been cursory at best. 'I've already blown the lid on what you're planning,' he said, fighting to keep his tone steady. 'It's over – whatever you do to me, your plan to blow up Manchester and JFK and those other airports is screwed.'

'Hey, Predrag!' Kanska looked over to the window as Abdul's former captive appeared. 'The kid believed you. He phoned in the faked confession like I said he would.'

'Too easy.' Predrag was training Felix's gun at Abdul. 'I was ready to brave torture, anything to make the confession convincing. But they have no stomach for it. One punch and a couple of threats!' He sneered. 'I thought the kid was stupid, but the Kurd's even worse – all I did was kick his ankles away and down he went.'

Felix's sinking feeling touched rock bottom. 'This was all a come-on?'

'We couldn't risk you being hurt before you'd helped us out.' A smile played around Kanska's lips. 'It was obvious that a British security agency knew something of our plans when Lili was placed under surveillance. Then a Western boy shows up in the mountains here, poking about in our hideaways.' He moved the gun barrel down over Felix's cheek as though caressing the flesh. 'You and your people have been getting far too close, boy. Which is why we've used you to send them off the track . . .'

'Predrag's whole story was a lie?'

'On the contrary, all Predrag said was true – save for the location of our bomb.'

Felix felt like his mountain sickness was coming back. 'Bomb? Not bombs?'

'With four target sites to go over across the globe, your organizations will have their hands well and truly full,' Kanska gloated. 'And inevitably, they will neglect the real and most obvious target – New Heathrow.'

Felix made no reply. He knew there was shedloads of security in place, ready for the reopening. What worried him was, Kanska had to know it too.

So why wasn't he bothered?

'I guess you're going to kill me,' Felix said.

'Not quite yet, little boy. The illusion you've created must be maintained.' Kanska smiled again. 'You are being tracked remotely, yes? And if your signal disappears now with four days to go before detonation, questions may be asked. So – you're coming to England with us.'

'Your people-smuggling operation?' Felix sneered.

'Effective in bringing all kinds of undesirables in and out of your country,' Kanska assured him. 'Myself included. I must be present for the final preparations of my nuclear device. I've allowed my little camera-crew recruitment drive to delay me longer than I'd wished, but since I couldn't risk smuggling them all, it was important to get good men with no criminal record, who will get into the country without arousing suspicion . . . ahead of the carnage to come.'

'Think of the people you'll kill,' said Felix, trying to force steel into his glare. 'Men, women, children—'

'I think of the children the most,' Kanska said softly. 'Children are the future. Destroy the children, you destroy that future.'

Felix forgot about the rifles pointing his way or the gun to his head. He lunged forward, hands hooked into talons to rake out the smug killer's throat. But Kanska dodged the clumsy attack. Felix grunted as a gun butt smacked down on the back of his head. His skull rang with red sparks and blackness came down over him.

. . . FIVE . . .

Brightness burned down on Felix as he woke and opened his sticky eyes. He winced as pain punched at the back of his head. When he could see again and had blinked away the glare of the sun he saw the smoke dying from a blackened pile of timbers in the shell of a building, twenty metres or so away. He must still be on the Blackmoon site. Abdul was now awake, on his knees in the dust with two M16s jammed up against his bruised face. His dark eyes were full of fear.

Kanska's gloating words echoed back to Felix in his memory. He wished he could keep his eyes closed, curl up and blot out everything. No amount of training could ever prepare him for making a screw-up like this.

'Contact your people.' His satphone was pressed roughly into his right hand by Predrag. To his left, Kanska sat in a canvas chair. He looked tired and pale.

Felix glared at the terrorist and let the phone fall from his hand.

'You will contact them, please,' Kanska said, like a patient teacher with a difficult pupil. 'Tell them that in order to escape your enemies you must take the place of another man in Orpheus's people-smuggling route out of Irbil. It will take four days. On the positive side, you are able to take Predrag with you for interrogation.'

Felix shook his head. In response, the click of the rifles' safeties were disengaged and Abdul whimpered as the barrels were jammed harder against his temples, turning the skin around them pale.

'You want me to explain my silence in the run-up to your bomb going off,' Felix said quietly. 'If I don't do it, I guess you'll kill Abdul and me. But if I do, you'll murder thousands, maybe millions of people – and the two of us as well.' He swallowed. 'I . . . I just can't do it.'

'Look into the eyes of your friend,' Kanska ordered. 'The lives of thousands? This is an abstract. You have no connection to those strangers. But two allies in adversity . . .'

'Let them kill me,' Abdul whispered, his voice breaking, eyes tightly shut. 'We're dead whatever happens, you said so yourself.'

'But he knows too that where there's life, there's hope – eh, Felix?' Kanska grinned like he'd just made a great joke. 'There's still four days to go. You could turn this around, right? A part of you is thinking this: *Surely ATLAS will discover there are no tunnels under these great airports inside of four days? That there is no trace of radioactivity?* You think too, perhaps, that in those four days, you may get the chance to overpower Predrag and me . . .'

'Abdul's right,' Felix said, forcing himself to stare into Predrag's eyes. 'You'll kill me as soon as I do what you want.'

'But I want you back in Britain, Felix,' Kanska insisted. 'My actions will bring the most important men and women in the intelligence service scurrying out of cover and into top-level meetings. My lensman crews will video the headquarters of your military agencies so we might identify these VIPs, and prepare for their subsequent assassination. And you, Felix – you shall be the assassin. You will meet with them, fitted with enough explosives to kill you all.'

Felix swore. 'So you didn't just want them to film the blast.'

Kanska didn't seem to have heard him, lost in his imaginings. 'Your superiors' final thoughts will be to know how absolutely they have failed. How completely Supyan Kanska outsmarted them.' He smiled again. 'There is an elegance to using their own unlikely agent against them, do you see? So don't make me kill you. You must hate me very badly, no? Let that hate sustain you. As I say, you may yet get the chance to kill me first, if—'

'All right,' Felix muttered. *Maybe the maniac's right*, he told himself. *Maybe I can turn this around further down the line.* 'All right, I'll do it.'

Kanska stayed smiling; the smug, sickening smile of a bad loser who knows that this time, he's won. 'I'm so pleased the Orpheus administration turned to me to lead this campaign.'

'I thought your fight was about power to the separatists, liberating the Russian republics?' said Felix. 'Getting independence for your family's oppressed homelands. How is destroying New Heathrow going to help that?'

'I assure you that in time it will be of the greatest benefit to my struggle.' Kanska smiled. 'Do please make the call.'

Keep stalling them. 'But what about that diagram Rashed was—'

'DO IT,' Kanska barked.

Predrag pushed the phone into Felix's hand again. This time, Felix gripped it. He looked at Abdul, who was staring miserably down at the floor.

I've got to turn this round.

'Remember,' Kanska warned him. 'Say only that to escape with Predrag you are taking the smugglers' route yourself. Do not attempt to tip your people off by giving an incorrect passcode – I memorized the one you gave earlier. Fail to convince and we kill not only your shamed friend Abdul but we will also set bombs at several local schools. The deaths will be down to you, Felix Smith.'

Felix felt like someone had thumped him in the guts. He wanted to hurl himself at the monsters around him. But he knew he had to stay calm and focused, to hold things together.

He dialled, and got the Girl; took a deep breath as she gave the usual non-greeting. He replied with his name and passcode. 'I don't have long,' Felix said tersely, and Predrag's gun nudged against his neck as if to remind him how true that was.

'You're still on site,' the Girl remarked.

'Couldn't get away as planned,' he said. 'Things are hot here but I think I can score the smugglers' escape route in the truck with my prisoner.' Kanska was holding up four fingers. 'It'll take four days, I think.'

'Four days?' The Girl sounded uneasy.

'Guess I'll miss New Heathrow's opening,' Felix remarked, and instantly felt the barrel bite hard against the back of his skull. He swallowed hard. 'But . . . got no choice. Only way out.'

'What about your conscious contact—'

'Abdul got away in my place, and you guys'll be able to talk to him any time,' Felix said quickly. 'He's staying with his cousin at the Wi-Fi café.' *There*, he thought, ignoring the cold look on his captors' faces and winking at his ally. *They won't dare neg Abdul now. Not if they think he might be contacted*.

The Girl paused. 'You think you can get home successfully this way?'

'I'm dead if I don't try,' he told her, licking his lips. 'Besides, you know me – I always know exactly what I'm doing. Out.'

Felix killed the connection, as Predrag swiped away the phone. Sweat was pouring from him. Would the Girl remember he'd admitted just the opposite before? Would she think anything of his crummy little clue about New Heathrow? If she only suspected he was being got at, she might question the story he had given and raise the alarm . . .

'You needn't have bothered about Abdul,' Predrag informed him. 'We need him alive for the same reason we need you. Don't want any alarm bells ringing. Not till the nuke goes off . . .'

'And go off it shall,' Kanska assured him. He glanced over as a large truck reversed into a warehouse across the builder's yard. 'Ah. Our transport has arrived. It will travel day and night, take us out through Turkey, into Bulgaria and all across Europe to the United Kingdom.'

'We'll be stuck in a truck for four days and nights?' Felix eyed the truck uneasily. 'What are we travelling with?'

'The consignment of materials has changed with each journey as our needs have changed. Sometimes mining equipment, or tunnel supports.' Kanska was clearly enjoying his chance to gloat. 'Even reactor-grade plutonium.'

Felix frowned. 'You've made a bomb using reactor-grade, not weapons-grade?'

'Reactor-grade is a lot easier and cheaper to get hold of.'

It's also a lot less predictable and a whole lot more dangerous, Felix thought, remembering training lectures. 'Those dead men in the back of the Toyota . . . and Rashed back in Britain.'

'The bomb we tested underground here detonated prematurely before the full yield of the explosion could be achieved. Exposure was inevitable . . .' Kanska nodded with a wan smile. 'I have had tests. It seems I too have contracted radiation sickness.'

'Your test took out an entire village,' Felix said coldly.

Kanska shrugged. 'There are many casualties of war, and I am one of them. I am dying. But I am not a bitter man.' The thin curl of his smile returned. 'It means I have nothing to lose by staying with my redesigned bomb until the last moment. To ensure that nothing goes wrong.'

Felix saw the fanaticism in the man's grey eyes. He wasn't relishing the thought of spending ninety-six hours with him in the back of a truck. Then suddenly Predrag jammed an injector against Felix's arm. Felix winced and snatched his arm away. But already he could feel the blur of whatever drug he'd been given softening his insides. He stumbled as his legs grew heavy. Abdul struggled up and stepped forward to grab him and help him stand. Guns were cocked and loaded, but Abdul kept holding on, his hands steadying Felix around his hips.

'Have a good, safe drive, Junior,' Abdul muttered. 'I'll have one too.' Then he was punched in the guts and dragged away at rifle point, spluttering for breath. Felix tried to speak but his tongue felt fat and dry, like it had no place in his mouth. He felt himself being roughly dragged through the dirt towards the waiting truck, then for the second time that day he kissed consciousness goodbye.

... FOUR ...

Felix woke with a start in the dark, he didn't know how much later. He'd had the dream of Day Zero again – watching his dad defusing the dummy devices, re-running the hideous footage of the jets erupting in smoke and fire, of the terminal tearing apart. He tried to calm his breathing, wanted to check his watch – but he couldn't move. He felt sluggish and sore, but was aware of vibration trembling through his bones. He supposed he was in the truck, driving through God knew where. He tried to move his right arm again and it came up short against thick plastic sheeting. Automatically he started to push against it, writhing to be free.

'Keep still.' Kanska's muffled, mannered English carried through the rustling murk. 'The airholes in the plastic tarpaulin about you are very carefully aligned to allow you to breathe. It's a kind of cocoon. But if you struggle, it will instead become your shroud. Wrapped up as we are, customs officers are unlikely to detect us. The downside, I'm afraid, is that with two of us in the truck there's a thirty per cent chance of us suffocating in transit.'

Felix didn't answer, fighting the surge of claustrophobia that threatened to swamp his senses. He was determined to show no fear or weakness in front of this maniac.

Still groggy, he forced himself to focus on the wider situation – *Before you can sort it, you have to make sense of it*. He remembered his instructors discussing the threat of terrorist organizations using nuclear bombs. Given a choice, such devices would be made using highly restricted weapons-grade plutonium – reactor-grade *could* be used but it was less stable and more radioactive – and thirty per cent more of it was required to achieve the same explosive yield as weapons-grade. In addition, reactor-grade plutonium gave off a lot more heat than its weapons-grade counterpart – five times as much if memory served – which made it a liability around the high explosive needed to trigger the device . . .

Kanska's voice insinuated itself through the thick swathes of plastic once more. 'If you turn your head you will find a tube that you can suck on for water. Dried food is accessed from the wider tube beside it.'

'I guess we won't be stopping for toilet breaks?'

'A commode has been placed beneath you and a catheter inserted . . .'

Felix winced as he became aware of discomfort down below. *At least it's safe to crap myself*, he thought darkly. *Thinking of which* . . .

'So your team has tunnelled under New Heathrow and placed a nuclear bomb down there, is that what we're talking about?'

No answer. Only rasping breaths.

'How have you got past the overheating problem with your plutonium?'

Again, Kanska gave no reponse.

It's a long journey, thought Felix. *I can wait*. He settled back stiffly in his cold plastic swaddling and hoped sleep would take him again soon.

Time became a sluggish blur. Captivity was driving Felix mad. Every minute brought the final catastrophe a tiny bit closer. And here he was, smothered, helpless. He was dimly aware of light penetrating his suffocating landscape; of another needle in the arm; of fitful, drug-induced sleep, with bad dreams that left him laced with sweat; and long, aching hours awake, breathing stale air in the darkness.

Predrag appeared to him once through the thick haze of plastic, reached in and snapped the Minos chain from around Felix's neck, pulling it away. 'We don't want ATLAS coming to meet us at Southampton docks, do we? So you're going off-radar for a time.'

Felix felt as though the last connection to his real life had been taken. He longed for his ordeal to be over, wanted to scream and shout for help and comfort. He thought of his dad, wondering what he would've done, and about the Girl. Had the fake testimony he'd given been too convincing? If so, then right now, Minos's resources could be stretched most ways round the world, when all the time in the south of England . . .

If only I'd been able to send Minos the portable hard disk. But it was in the pocket of his cargo pants, and they must have been removed from him when he was being prepped for the long haul across Europe. If there were details of deliveries to the Heathrow area somewhere on the cloned network, it might have alerted someone to what was really happening. But now . . .

He moistened his lips with the last of the water through his straw. How long had they been travelling? Felix knew that about the only advantage he had was that he was young and fit, while Kanska was sick and past his prime. The man had to be weakening now, surely? If he could be goaded into letting something slip . . .

'I don't see how you expect this one attack to break us,' Felix said loudly. 'Didn't you work it out after Day Zero? Whatever you inflict on us in the West, it only makes us that much tougher, that much more determined to beat you.'

'An infantile response,' Kanska wheezed. 'Attack shall follow attack, wearing you down, breeding discontent. Extremist groups will gain a voice. American and European unity will fall apart as each once-great power turns inwards to lick its wounds.'

'Yeah, well,' Felix said, taking a deep stale breath and going for the bluff of his life. 'That diagram we found on Rashed – the one marking the positions of your lensmen so they can film the blast. We've worked out the over-watch positions. It took a while, but we've found the matching skyline.'

'Is that so?'

'Yes.' Felix prayed the dying man would rise to the bait. 'You know it is.'

'I know you are lying,' Kanska retorted. 'The diagram does not show buildings.'

'Of course it does,' Felix persisted. *You want me to play dumb? I'll play dumb. Anything so long as you tell me something that could help make a difference.* 'You just hate it that we worked it out.'

Kanska snorted. 'The diagram doesn't show pillars of stone and glass reaching up into the sky. It shows deep, deep shafts in the rock *beneath* west London.'

'Beneath?' The whispered word seemed to bounce back at Felix, hollow and dead.

'We've done far more than drive a tunnel under the airport to emplace the bomb and get us in and out of the strike zone.' *At last*, thought Felix, as Kanska's inner braggard was set free into the stifling darkness. 'Orpheus had compromised one of the building contractors long before they were awarded the contract to re-lay the foundations of Heathrow. The diagram you found, when overlaid on one in my keeping, displays key strategic sites all over west London where vents to the surface have been tunnelled out; a map by which our video crews can set remote cameras ready for their coverage of the airport's "grand reopening" . . .'

'Vents in the ground?'

'Why allow so much of the blast to be absorbed by solid rock, when we can channel such power to the surface?' Kanska's laugh gave way to a wheezing cough.

'Not only will New Heathrow be torn apart from beneath, but the power of the firestorm will be channelled along the shafts to the world above . . .'

'No . . .' Felix's guts churned as the full implication of what he was hearing filtered through his senses. 'Great big holes in the ground? They'd have been found.'

'Most emerge into private land acquired by our supporters – land where we have dumped a good deal of the excavated bedrock from these tunnels. And do you really think it wouldn't occur to us to conceal the other openings?' Kanska coughed again noisily. 'Tons of radioactive debris will be spat into the atmosphere. The streets will be buried in ash. Poisonous particles will gust through the capital and beyond, until the fallout comes down in a deadly rain, polluting and killing . . . And soon the whole world will see the proof of it, with footage shot long-distance from a dozen angles.'

Felix listened to the voice drone on and wished he could cover his ears, that he'd never started this. 'You're giving Orpheus a way to hold the entire world to ransom.'

'The greater powers that seek so desperately to suppress smaller nations and steal their wealth and resources will at last know what it is to be persecuted, to be dictated to.' Kanska wheezed for breath. 'I suspect that your government will take Orpheus's foreign policy demands more seriously in future. And Moscow shall heed those of the North Caucasus separatists, as the men who succeed me fight on to free my homeland from Russian rule . . .'

'You walked out on that fight,' Felix jeered. 'Sold out to Orpheus.'

'Generous donations of funding and manpower will be made to my cause upon successful detonation of the device,' Kanska revealed, and Felix could hear the smile in his voice. 'I had the vision and the know-how, but not the resources to make it a reality.'

But Orpheus did . . . thought Felix. He wished he could tear at the thick plastic sheets around him, get free and get to Kanska, stop him and silence him for ever. But the terrorist's words lingered in the stale air like fallout. After days of freezing darkness trying to get the man to speak, Felix found he had never known what darkness truly meant – until now.

'It will all be over soon, boy,' Kanska muttered, exhaustion cracking through his feeble voice. 'All of it.'

... THREE ...

Reality washed in on Felix as he woke up in his boxers, freezing cold on a concrete floor. Someone was dousing him with icy water from a high-pressure hose, drowning the stink of four days' nightmare travel. His limbs were cramped and pressure sores on his back stung in the foaming deluge. He got to his knees, rubbed his hands through his hair, swallowed some of the water thirstily, willing his throbbing head to clear as he tried to take in his surroundings.

He was in a warehouse, a cavernous shell of a building. Strip-lights glared down. A dozen or so men stood about checking camcorders, tripods and lenses, while another did the honours with the hose. They spoke a language Felix couldn't fathom, and he noted the guns beneath their fluorescent builders' jackets. Kanska's loyal lensmen. Beyond them stood the same truck he had seen at Blackmoon Construction, now sporting British licence plates. Parked to the left of a large loading-bay door was a collection of nondescript cars and vans.

To his left, the space was piled high with a jumble of building supplies; chunks of cast concrete and tunnel props formed a ramshackle wall dividing the rest of the warehouse from a makeshift workshop – three trestle tables covered with tools and electronic equipment. With a stab of surprise, Felix recognized his own rucksack leaning against an oil-stained generator. Kanska or Predrag must've taken it from Abdul's taxi and brought it along – presumably to exploit its contents for counter-intel purposes.

'All right, he's had his shower.' It was Predrag who spoke, dressed in a sharp black suit, a bundle of clothing in one hand and a revolver in the other. 'He's wide awake now.'

Felix shivered miserably with cold. He clocked a handful of other men, tough-looking, armed and swarthy, standing behind Predrag. If he ran now, he wouldn't stand a chance. 'Where are we?'

'Outside Heathrow. But some of my mercenaries here will drive you to Manchester shortly.' Predrag tossed over a small, grubby towel and a pair of brown overalls. 'Once we're there, you'll make a call they can trace confirming the bomb is concealed at the airport. We want ATLAS to be certain the threat is well away from London – don't want them getting nervous and postponing the grand opening of New Heathrow, do we?'

Slowly Felix's mind worked around the timings. *It was*

the weekend when we left, and we've had four nights in the truck . . . 'Is it Wednesday today?'

'Just about ten hours now until the opening ceremony of New Heathrow.'

Felix's heart jumped as though shot. The man with the hose sniggered as he turned off the tap. 'I reckon the royal speech will bring the house down.'

There were guffaws from some of the men, others just smirked. The mercenaries looked blank, hovering behind Predrag, waiting for instructions. As Felix dried himself off he felt colder than ever. 'So then what? You lock me up till you've identified your targets and set me loose to blow them up?'

'Something like that,' Predrag agreed, but Felix hardly heard him. He was wondering if his rifle was still in his rucksack.

'I see you've noticed we've brought your pack along.' Kanska had emerged from the back of the truck, looking scrawnier than ever in blue jeans and a white polo neck. 'Soon, we shall fill it with high explosives. When you go to the rendezvous with your handlers, the pack will be secured to your back.' He smiled. 'We could have made you wear one of our special fishing vests as dear Lili did, but this way, your body shape remains unaltered and suspicions will not be aroused . . .'

'And what if I yell the place down?' Felix muttered, pulling on the overalls.

Predrag turned to Kanska and tutted. 'The boy thinks we're going to leave him with a tongue in his head.'

Felix felt a surge of fear. Again he assessed the

general strength and fitness of the armed men he'd have to get through to escape. It seemed impossible. He stood up, wincing as agonizing pain clamped hold of his calf muscles, and staggered towards the stack of concrete, closer to his pack. The mercenaries twitched into life; guns were pulled and safeties clicked off.

'Cramp,' Felix protested.

'Ah, yes. You are dehydrated, it is to be expected, no?' Kanska splashed over the wet floor, Predrag following at his heels like a lapdog. Felix turned to face them gingerly. 'You think we can't see the way you're taking in everything, hoping for your chance to run?' Kanska smiled sympathetically. 'Ah, cruel hope. Hope that one shall overcome even the greatest odds – it is difficult to crush, isn't it?' He nodded to himself. 'I see that I shall have to break you. And let me assure you, boy – hands, unlike hopes, crush easily.'

Felix gasped as Predrag grabbed hold of his wrists and forced his hands flat against the concrete. 'Don't!' The armed men in the fluorescent vests gathered round, eager to see. One of them watched through the viewfinder of his camcorder. 'You don't need to do this!'

'I know. But I told you, I hate the children worst of all.' Kanska motioned to one of the mercenaries, who stepped forward and raised his assault rifle, letting the butt hover over Felix's knuckles. 'Which would you rather he pulverized first, Felix – the left hand or the right?'

Panting with fear, Felix clenched his fists tight. 'Not got the bottle to do it yourself?'

A sadistic smile played round Kanska's gaunt face. 'There's a better view from here.'

Felix struggled desperately in Predrag's iron grip. Mercenaries and lensmen together cheered him on sarcastically in Slavic-sounding accents. Kanska smiled as the man he'd chosen made ready to slam down the rifle with shattering force . . .

Then Felix jerked his head back hard into Predrag's face. Caught by surprise, Predrag loosened his grip enough for Felix to slip free and elbow him in the guts. The mercenary swung the rifle round to cover his prisoner – but Felix was already throwing Predrag over his shoulder to land hard against his would-be torturer, and both men staggered blindly into Kanska. Cameras were dropped and fists and guns raised as the watching men rushed towards him. Felix turned and started to sprint away, but his co-ordination was shot after so long cramped in captivity, and he slipped on the wet floor. The men fanned out to encircle Felix, cutting off his escape – as Predrag pushed past two of them to get to him first . . . .

Suddenly the heavy loading-bay doors were smashed apart as a huge truck crashed into the entrance. Felix hurled himself to the ground as the armed men turned in alarm to find soldiers rushing in alongside the truck, sporting tinted visors and respirators; they looked to Felix to be ATLAS hostage-rescue troops. Then a series of stun grenades went off, their blinding plumes of magnesium whiteness filling the space with a deafening cacophony of booms which all but drowned out the abrasive clatter of gunfire.

For a split second Felix was as stunned and disoriented as anyone else in the room. But then he remembered Hannah and the Girl, and knew that a split second was all he had.

Desperately Felix rolled over and over for the shelter of the concrete slabs that bordered the work area. Howling screams tugged at his ringing ears. Glancing back, he grimaced to find two bogus builders sprawled lifeless on the floor, slotted where they stood – and four neat crimson holes in Predrag's chest. Caught in plain sight, the terrorist thug had become an instant target. He sank to his knees, clawing his way in agony towards the cover of the workbenches, as the mercenaries and the remaining lensmen raced for cover behind cars and vans and began returning fire with their own weapons. One must have decided Felix made an easier target, unleashing a spray of bullets in his direction. The concrete spat shrapnel over Felix as he pressed himself flat on the floor and dragged himself out of sight behind the pile.

As he did so, he saw Predrag's body slumped underneath a table – but there was no sign of Kanska. The overlord had disappeared.

Swearing, Felix looked anxiously around. There were no obvious exit points in sight. So unless Kanska was a magician as well as a maniac, he had to still be here, surely . . .

There was a brief lull in the gunfire as more ATLAS troops stormed into the warehouse. One was taken down immediately, but more soldiers quickly joined them, fanning out through the warehouse, taking cover behind crates.

With a thrill of euphoria, Felix sighted Zane among them. Not just a handler, then. He took active service too. But then ATLAS had always played fast and loose with the rules – why else was Felix here.

But how the hell did Zane find me?

Right now, the answer to that question had to take a back seat to simple survival. Felix snatched up his ruck-sack, crawled under the table and shoved some sandbags in his way aside to reveal a large, metal inspection hatch – like a manhole cover – built clumsily into the warehouse floor just ahead of him.

Explains Kanska's disappearing act. And at once, Felix knew that this hatch must lead down to one of the Orpheus tunnels.

Kanska had gone to his bomb.

Felix scrabbled desperately at the hatch but it was jammed tight – most likely locked from the inside. The only way through would be to blow it open.

All things considered, good job I'm sitting in a bomber's workshop.

He would have to make a breaching charge.

Felix cautiously knelt up and surveyed the materials scattered across the table. He grabbed two sticks of PE4 plastic explosive and some detonating cord. Trying to shut out the brain-pounding soundtrack of screams and whistling bullets, he took a metre of cord and sliced through it – it looked just like a length of electric cable, except in place of wire there was powdered PETN high explosive. Then Felix picked up the PE4 and started moulding it around the cord, arranging it into a block the size of a DS.

A stray bullet slammed into the table and split the wood, jolting him backwards. Fighting to keep cool, working as quickly as he dared, he reached for a reel of black gaffer-tape on the floor and tore off enough to cover the explosive – then attached the detonator to the tail of det cord protruding from the tape. Finally he rigged the taped bundle to an M3 pull/release firing device – one of several trigger options littering the floor and tables. It wasn't his finest work, but given the situation . . .

With the warehouse still thumping and shrieking with the sounds of battle, Felix scuttled back behind the concrete and placed the charge flat against the steel inspection cover. Then he carefully attached the M3's detonator and unreeled its tripwire attachment, making for the cover of the workbench where Predrag's lifeless body now lay – a crimson trail showed he'd dragged himself several metres from the place he'd been shot. Peering out towards the parked vehicles, he saw another of the lensmen lying dead in a pool of blood – and a mercenary emerging from inside one of the white vans with grenades.

Felix yelled out a warning to Zane and the others but even his loudest shout couldn't carry over the din of covering fire. The mercenary pitched his grenade and it went off, blowing the front of the ATLAS truck apart and blasting metal and glass into the ranks of the troops. Two soldiers were sent reeling into the open, where their bodies danced and spat blood under gunfire.

Sickened, scared half to death, Felix screamed another warning to the ATLAS troops and yanked hard on the trip-wire to detonate the charge. The blast shook the warehouse as a column of flame and smoke leaped into the air from behind the pile of building supplies. With no time to wait, Felix crawled out of hiding to check the hatch cover – only to find one of the ATLAS troops shooting at him as well in the smoke and confusion, mistaking him for the enemy.

'Friendly! Friendly!' Felix yelled helplessly. 'Just a breaching charge!' Bullets tore apart the concrete around him. But then the Orpheus man hurled another grenade into the ATLAS ranks and Zane and the other men fell back in a flare of smoke and flame. The gunfire grew more sporadic, and Felix crawled towards the smoking hole he'd just put in the floor, ready to descend into whatever lay beneath . . .

A shadow fell over him.

With a spasm of fear Felix saw that Predrag had risen from the blood-soaked floor and was tottering towards him like something out of a horror film, his body a crimson mess. Retching for breath, the gory figure grabbed for Felix's throat with blood-slicked hands.

... TWO ...

Felix fell backwards, fighting to break Predrag's grip. He felt himself blacking out. *Can't let him stop me.* In desperation, he slapped both hands down hard on Predrag's ears, hoping to puncture the man's eardrums. His head spinning, he slapped even harder, again and again. With a groan, Predrag rolled off Felix and tumbled down through the shattered inspection hatch. As he did so, a pillar of fire shot up from the pit in the ground and the building shook with the force of an earthquake.

Kanska booby-trapped the tunnel entrance, Felix realized. *That could've been me.*

Then he glimpsed movement from the corner of his eye. The huge pile of moulded concrete slabs, no doubt weakened by the breaching charge, was now toppling over in the shockwave. Desperately, Felix tried to roll aside.

Too slow.

He screamed as the edge of a ten-centimetre-thick slab slammed down on the knuckles of his right hand. With a strength born of fear he managed to lift the slab and pull his bad hand free – a bloody, swollen mess. Horrified, Felix fought the bile rising in his throat. *Kanska wanted me crippled and he got it.*

But the bomb-maker still had to be stopped.

Almost weeping with the pain, Felix held his broken hand to his chest and pulled his respirator from his ruck-sack, glad that at least his kit seemed undisturbed. He secured the respirator round his face with his left hand, then threw his pack down into the abyss. There was so much smoke it was difficult to see clearly – a blessing, now the walls must be decorated with Predrag – but he caught a shine of silver in the blackness, an aluminium ladder leading down into the depths. It looked scorched and twisted. Could it bear his weight?

Even as he asked himself the question, Felix was scrambling down into the darkness. He realized he knew next to nothing about the Orpheus tunnels – how far did they extend under the ground? How many shafts led to the surface, ready to vent the radioactive debris, rather than to the bomb itself? He pictured himself wandering lost through the tunnels, getting further and further away from his goal while Kanska breezed straight there. Did the terrorist need to arm the bomb manually? Or had the countdown already been set in motion and was he stay-ing simply to go out in a blaze of glory, guarding against any would-be heroes mad enough to tackle his creation?

Would-be heroes like me, thought Felix bitterly, his hand throbbing with pain. *I should've warned Zane, got him to send the troops down here. But with them busy waging war on the lensmen posse . . .*

Hold it together, Smith. You're on your own.

The distant chatter of guns above ground grew slowly fainter as Felix descended. Soon he reached the last half-severed rung of the ladder. A pile of debris gouged out by the blast formed a precarious slope down to solid ground. But then he paused, holding dead still at the sound of movement ahead. Had Predrag survived the blast, or . . .

No. After four days trapped in the dark with it, Felix would've recognized the wheeze and rasp of Kanska anywhere. *Come to see who's fallen into your tripwires, huh?* His heart was hacking at his ribs as he listened to his opponent draw cautiously closer. Adrenaline dulled the pain in his hand. He held his breath and tensed every muscle, straining to make the first glimpse of his target . . .

The top of Kanska's bald head showed suddenly in the smoky light thrown down through the hatch; a shiny pink target hovering as he inspected the fallen rucksack. With a bellowed war cry, Felix jumped down from the ladder. Kanska looked up and found Felix's heel in his eye. He shouted out as he was kicked backwards into the darkness beyond – but Felix yelled louder as he landed awkwardly on the rubble pile and jarred his broken hand. He almost passed out with the pain, had to will himself to stay conscious. But then a fist collided with his jaw, knocked him sideways. Felix glimpsed Kanska's ghoulish face leering down at him, twisted with hatred. Teeth gritted, chunks of stone digging into his spine, Felix brought his foot up against Kanska's chest and propelled the man away. Then he slid himself awkwardly down the rock pile into the gloomy, stifling tunnel beyond it and hurled himself at the fallen terrorist.

But Kanska had drawn his gun. Without thinking, Felix tried to knock it away with his wrecked hand. The pain tore through him and he shrieked. Aware now of his enemy's weakness, Kanska grabbed hold of Felix's broken fingers and bent them backwards, jamming the gun under his chin.

'No!' Felix barked, elbowing Kanska's gun aside and headbutting him in the face. Kanska broke away, blood pouring down over his lips. Felix kicked the gun from his grip and punched him hard in the face. Kanska's head smacked against a scaffolding pole tunnel prop with a dull, hollow, chime. His eyes rolled back in his head and he sank to the ground.

Felix watched him, panting for breath, the harshness of the sound strangely deadened by the thick earthen walls of the tunnel.

Snatching up the gun, Felix stared down at Kanska, blood pounding through his temples and leaking from his fingers. *I ought to kill you*, he thought. *Kill you while you sleep. It wouldn't be murder, it would be an execution. No one would know . . .*

Felix spat on the floor. *Only, I'd know. I'd know then that I'm no better than you.* He stared into the darkness of the tunnel ahead. *And right now I need to be better*

*than you, if I'm going to beat the clock – and you with it.
If.*

He quickly stripped Kanska of the polo neck, pulled the man's arms behind him and tied the man's wrists to the tunnel prop. Then he hurried to his rucksack. Using his teeth and his good hand, Felix fished inside for his flashlight. Thank God no one had got around to emptying it yet . . .

He hesitated, felt a twinge of panic. *What am I thinking? Look at me. I've got a smashed hand, I'm not thinking straight. Do I really imagine I can step into Dad's shoes and live to walk away in them?*

He had to get back to Zane. Zane would be able to get a proper bomb disposal expert, someone with more experience, with two working hands. But as he made to scale the ladder, the screams of dying men floated eerily down to him. Men from which side? Kanska had fewer men but they were well armed and the mercenaries in particular clearly well trained. If the good guys were losing up there . . .

Swearing loudly, Felix picked up his pack, swung it carefully onto his shoulder and flicked on the flashlight. He could see faint footprints in the hard-packed soil – they had to have been made by Kanska or one of his cronies.

Felix followed the tunnel along, focusing on the ground ahead of him, searching it out for any abnormality, the tiniest warning sign that a trap might lie ahead.

Absorbed as he was, Felix wasn't sure how far he'd trailed through the dark, claustrophobic tunnels. The air tasted earthy and stale, despite the occasional venting tunnel overhead, sloping away to a concealed opening in the surface. How close to Heathrow Airport were they now? He realized the vents served a double purpose – letting in air from above for Kanska and his team, as well as giving easy passage for the firestorm.

Onwards Felix went, further and deeper, through the passage as it wound through the bedrock. The tunnel was completely silent save for the furtive tread of his footsteps. The tracks led on and on. The pack was getting heavier on his shoulder, his busted hand was throbbing fit to fall off and the lack of oxygen was worsening his headache. To top it all, his torchlight was failing. He quickened his step, tried to breathe evenly and not deplete the oxygen further.

Then, suddenly, he stopped. In the dim torchlight he could see more footprints, the faint indentations pointing in different directions. Straight away Felix's unease flared into full-on Spidey-sense – *danger ahead*. Something had happened here, or somewhere further up. A trap. It was time to put on the brakes and figure out what lay ahead . . .

But how much time did he have left?

The passage remained dark and deathly silent. Giving up on the flashlight, Felix carefully laid down his rucksack and pulled out his night-vision monocle, gingerly fastening it over his head and clunking the lens firmly into place over his right eye. He began to scan the area, first with his exposed eye, then through the scope, using its infrared laser as a spotting device for anything unusual.

Slowly, methodically, he took another couple of tentative steps forward and scanned all around again. *Ten metres in two minutes*, he thought anxiously. *This is hopeless . . .*

Then he stopped dead as he caught a faint flash of light through the infrared night-vision equipment, and made out a vague but visible shadow, just above floor level.

It was a tripwire; the thread was reflecting the infrared laser back at him.

Taking his entire bodyweight on one arm, Felix carefully dropped down to the floor and slowly began edging himself forward until he was less than a hand's reach away from the deadly length of nylon thread. By carefully focusing on the scope's pale green sight-picture he was just about able to make out where it joined the circuit. One end of the wire was fastened to a girder on the opposite side of the tunnel, while the other had been inserted through the end of a microswitch arm, itself attached to a small black box – the triggering unit. Two wires were protruding from the far side of the box and trailing off into the distance . . . presumably to the nuke.

Jesus, he thought, the sweat practically gushing down his back. The slightest pressure against the tripwire would pull the microswitch shut and it would be game over – for most of London.

Lucky these overalls are already brown.

Felix took a deep breath, then, reaching back into his rucksack, carefully removed his snips. He edged the blades up to the tripwire, closed his eyes and squeezed the jaws shut.

The golden sound of absolute silence followed the cut.

Scratch one booby trap, he thought, and placed the snips in the pocket of his overalls.

What else was waiting? *Let's bring it on.*

Picking up his pack, he climbed back to his feet and resumed his slow shuffle into the unknown. The tunnel was bitterly cold. He could feel the drumbeat of his heart and the pulse of pain through his hand. Thoughts of how the nuke might be constructed raced through his mind. *How big is it? How will it be encased? Even if I reach the thing, will I be able to cut into it?*

As he started to pick up the pace, shining the invisible laser back and forth while scanning for further tripwires, some kind of gut instinct suddenly told him to stop. Warily he began scanning the area from his static position.

And then he saw it: on the edge of one of the shoring beams about twenty metres in front of him he could see a black box – no bigger than a packet of cigarettes – and its tiny white lens aperture.

It was a passive infrared sensor, designed to react to body heat. Felix swore. They were almost completely impossible to defeat . . .

. . . almost.

Felix shook off his pack and started to rummage with his good hand for the one bit of kit that might be able to save him – the foil blanket he'd last used in the Iraqi mountains. Such blankets were supposed to help conserve body heat . . .

Quickly unfolding the blanket, Felix eyed the PIR. 'Let's see how good they are at it.' With some difficulty, working one-handed, he covered himself completely, cutting the tiniest of slits to see through.

He stood there astride his pack, sweating in the darkness, checking that the hem of the foil now rested on the ground all the way around him – and suddenly realized quite how surreal the entire situation had become. Here he was, dressed like a silver foil lampshade, attempting to neutralize the biggest, baddest IED ever used by terrorists.

He thought back to his dad's words: *The truth is stranger than fiction*. Now he knew exactly what he meant. You really couldn't make this stuff up. He pressed on, nudging his rucksack along with his feet, the sound of his laboured breathing drowned out by the rustling of his protective cowl. He kept his clear eye closed, squinting out through the eerie green of the night-vision lens. He knew that with each shuffled step, the danger doubled. As his heart hammered away like a pneumatic drill, the blanket was starting to feel more like concrete than foil.

After what seemed like a lifetime, he drew up beneath the small black plastic sensor box. It was tilted slightly down; an all-seeing eye, poised, alert and waiting to react.

Once again Felix reached down into his kitbag. Only this time he removed a ceramic knife – which he held between his teeth – and a small circuit-detector box, which he held clamped under his arm. Then he extended the blade through the slit in the blanket poncho, praying that he didn't expose his fingers . . . the smallest flash of human tissue was enough for a PIR to respond.

Slowly, carefully, he reached up to the PIR's sheathed wiring circuit with the knife and began scraping away at the sheath's outer core. Once the four wires inside had been exposed, he put the blade back between his teeth, forced his circuit-detector box through the slit in the foil, held it to the wires and used the knife blade to switch it to 'Run'.

Blinking away the sweat, he saw the box's quartz screen was telling him to cut the second and fourth wires.

Swapping the box for his snips, he moved them as close to the contour of the wall as he could and cut the PIR out of the bomb's circuit. With a shaky sigh of relief, he spat out the knife and ripped the foil blanket away, breathing in the stale, cold air in deep, ragged breaths.

Two down.

Then, as he set off again cautiously into the tunnel, Felix saw a faint glow up ahead. Walking as if through a bad dream, he found the tunnel opened up into a gigantic cylindrical cavern, lit by similar lanterns to those in the cave outside Dahuk. It was as big as a football stadium. Huge holes in the high ceiling could only be the vents Kanska had gloated about, ready to share the nuclear love with the population above.

And Felix could've sworn his heart actually stopped beating as he spotted a suitcase, positioned on one of the crossbeams helping to support the cavern roof.

The bomb.

... ONE ...

I'm standing next to a nuclear bomb for God's sake, with next to no shielding. It could explode at any moment.

Felix had to fight an urge to turn and run. Finally he was facing the IED that, if it went off, would make the events of Day Zero look like an end-of-the-news filler. And who was London's great defender? A fifteen-year-old with a flattened hand.

He heard Hannah's voice in his ears. *You really think you're Mr High-and-Mighty, don't you? Felix Smith, coming to save the world single-handed.*

'You betcha,' Felix breathed. 'Let's do this.'

The bomb was in a bastard of a position, virtually impossible to get to without the right gear, let alone with one hand. But since there was no one about to moan to, he mustered all his strength, reached over his head and did a one-handed pull-up, heaving himself onto the nearest girder. Panting for breath, he swung his legs up and twisted his body so that he was lying on top of the studded metal bar. He shimmied along the hard surface, trying to ignore the pain in his hand and the rasp of the rivets against his skin, edging closer to the bomb.

'I've come a long way to meet you,' he murmured to the suitcase. 'Frankly, I wish I hadn't bothered.'

Moments later he was hunched beside it, his legs clamped round the girder. Carefully keeping his balance, he slipped off his pack and hooked one of the straps over the end of the joist. It allowed him to reach into the rucksack with relative freedom, and soon he had located and removed the portable Goldman X-ray generator. He used to joke about the thing in training – it looked more like a hairdryer than a high-tech piece of equipment. He placed the device against the edge of the nuke and, using the elbow of his bad arm, switched it to 'active'. Moments later, he was contouring around the suitcase, studying its contents via the small, high-definition screen.

Felix hated what he saw, but at least he could under-stand it. He made out a large battery, an arming switch and the firing switches, a digital countdown timer, a photo slave-cell and a mercury tilt-switch. The timer was the primary trigger and the latter two switches were obviously designed to cause the device to detonate if it was opened or moved.

How long do I have?

He continued scanning the suitcase device and quickly

identified a large sphere surrounded by a shedload of explosive, all linked by a nest of wiring interconnected to printed circuit boards. The sphere contained the unstable reactor-grade plutonium – no doubt about it. Precision-drawn aluminium tubes had been attached, presumably as a cooling system to drain some of the excess heat, a stab at making it slightly safer.

'Guess we're in business,' Felix murmured. On the upside, he now knew exactly what he was dealing with. The downside was that it was the most complex device he could imagine . . . an implosion-triggered nuclear fission bomb.

Felix swallowed and it felt as though he had a brick in his throat. *This is seriously old school*, he thought. Fat Man, the A-bomb that destroyed Nagasaki at the end of World War Two, was implosion powered. Essentially, the explosive detonated, sending shockwaves into the sphere powerful enough to compress the plutonium, doubling its density and so starting a nuclear chain reaction – resulting in an underground blast that would most likely cause most of Heathrow to cave in on itself. The vents would channel the horrific temperatures to the surface. Millions of people would die from burns, injuries and radiation.

He felt suddenly tiny in the cold, cavernous space.

It's time I started.

Felix decided to cut into the suitcase. Once he'd neutralized the firing switches, he'd be able to dis-assemble the bomb by hand. Literally.

He took a white marker pen from an inside pocket of

the rucksack and stuck it in his mouth like a cigar. Then, using the X-ray generator, he checked the location of the mercury tilt-switch and the photocell and marked their position by leaning forward and drawing with his mouth. Cutting into one of those by mistake was not a good plan. The fabric of the case smelled smoky and old. *Sweet Jesus*, he thought, *I'm practically kissing an A-bomb. How much radiation am I getting off this thing? How sick could I get?*

Like the long-term matters now.

Next, he marked the location of the clock, deciding to come in from the side and attack that first. He knew it was in there, but of course the X-ray couldn't tell him the time on the clock – one of its limitations. Felix had no idea how many hours or minutes he had left.

He wiped beads of sweat from his brow, turned to replace the Goldman in his pack, then carefully removed the rotary cutting tool from his pack and inched its spinning blade slowly towards the case. With surgical skill, he began carving into the plastic and soon had cut three neat incisions in the side of the case – effectively forming three sides of a square . . .

'NO!'

The shout raked through Felix like talons, making him jump and lose his balance. On instinct he grabbed hold of the timber to support himself with his shattered hand – and the pain was enough to jar the cutting tool from his grip. It fell with a clatter to the hard-packed earth below.

Felix looked back to find Kanska pointing at him from the mouth of the tunnel, bruised and livid with anger, accompanied by one of his mercenary lensmen who even now was raising his M16 for the killing shot.

'Wait, you fool.' Kanska batted the rifle down. 'You might hit the bomb.' He staggered towards Felix. 'Have you harmed it? Well? Answer me, you little—'

'Oh, I'll answer you,' Felix muttered through gritted teeth, the pain blinding as he groped desperately in his rucksack for his G36. 'Should've negged you when I had the chance.'

'Get him down,' Kanska snapped. His associate had produced a knife, and drew back his arm to throw. Felix pulled out the assault rifle, twisted his body round to bring it to bear – but he was too slow. The knife flashed in the dim light and struck him in the thigh, slicing deep into the flesh. Felix screamed out in pain as the rifle followed his cutter to the ground.

'Idiot,' Kanska spat at his companion. 'How many throws will it take?'

'No more,' the man promised, walking heavily towards Felix.

Felix gritted his teeth. He could feel hot blood soaking the leg of his overalls. With his good arm locked around the timber he couldn't even pull out the knife blade and staunch the bleeding. But if he dropped to the ground now he would stand no chance. And all the time, the bomb beside him was ticking away, brimful of unstable plutonium, ready to bring on Armageddon . . .

The man drew closer, smiling grimly, taking careful aim with his gun. Felix heard a sound like a dripping tap; realized it was blood from his leg striking the mud below.

It can't end this way. It mustn't. Sick with panic and pain, he turned helplessly to the blank, black face of the suitcase bomb. *I'm sorry, Dad. If I'd only been given just a few minutes more . . .*

A shot echoed out. Felix's eyes widened.

The man with the gun teetered over and fell face down in the mud, a bloody hole in his back.

Kanska spun round to confront his accomplice's killer in the mouth of the tunnel – in time to catch an entire clipful of bullets. His skinny body jerked and spun in the volley of shots, and when it finally fell, there was no getting up again.

A dark, bloodstained figure strode out of the tunnel. It was Zane. 'Targets neutralized,' he announced. Then his impassive face softened just a touch. 'Now get on and do your job, Felix.'

'Gotcha,' Felix said weakly, already heaving himself back round to face the bomb. He had to shut out his euphoria at his last-second rescue, to blank out the pain in his leg and his hand and just nail this bomb. Reaching into the rucksack, trying to calm his breathing, he pulled out a set of tweezers and carefully peeled back the small square panel exposing the clock's digital display. Now at last he would know how long he had before—

Fifty seconds.

Oh my God. He stared, willing it not to be true. *This just isn't happening.*

Normally he'd carry out detailed diagnostics on a circuit like this. Determine exactly which wires to cut. But that would take time and there was no way he could do it in fifty seconds. No way on earth.

His instructor's voice rang in his ears: *No short cuts!*

But there was no choice. He was going to have to take the world's greatest gamble.

Least I won't have time to bleed to death.

'How long we got?' Zane called.

'Bags of time,' Felix replied.

'You shitting me?'

'Yes.'

'Thought so. Appreciate that.'

'You're welcome.' Felix took his snips and carefully poked them into the case. Looking into the cavity as he did so, he located the four wires leading from the clock into one of the printed circuit boards and edged the blade against the first wire. He hesitated. *Which one is it, Dad?*

But there was no answer, of course. No divine guidance or last-moment flash of inspiration.

Thirty seconds. He tasted sick at the back of his throat. *This is insane*. But he knew he had no choice. It was now or never.

'Make a wish,' he called to Zane.

'I wish you knew what the hell you were doing,' Zane said dryly.

'You and me both . . .' Felix shut his eyes and squeezed the snips shut. Heard a taut, quiet twang as the first wire severed.

Nothing.

Twenty-three seconds.

Oh my God, oh my God. Felix moved the snips and

edged the blade towards a second wire. He knew he had a one in three chance of cutting the right one and rendering the timer inoperable. But if he was wrong, it was Apocalypse Now. A catastrophe from which the country would never recover.

Fourteen seconds. His own blood was ticking off the time in sticky drips.

'You can do it, Felix,' Zane told him, his voice steady. *Please, Dad, let this be the right wire.*

He breathed out, shook the sweat from his eyes one more time. Eased the tip of the cutters forward. Closer. Closer, until they were touching the wire. Focusing hard, aware only of the steady beat of his heart, he opened his palm and then gently squeezed the jaws shut.

He felt rather than heard the wire snap.

Then nothing.

Felix didn't dare to release the breath he was holding for quite some time.

'Are we good?' Zane called tensely.

Felix nodded in disbelief. 'We're better than we were.' Dizziness washed through him – euphoria or blood-loss, he wasn't sure. 'The timer's taken care of, but the bomb's still live.' *And with reactor-grade plutonium giving out so much heat, even with the aluminium conductors as a safeguard, there was no time to leave the device. It could still detonate at any moment.* He had to tackle the photocell next.

Grimly Felix started to search in his rucksack for his scalpel, but his vision was beginning to blur. *Screw the scalpel. Improvise.* He reached down to his leg, set his teeth together and yanked out the knife blade. The pain burned right the way through him, and the blood began to pour freely.

'Are you peeing yourself?' Zane demanded.

'No, but you should be.' Wiping the blood from the blade on his overalls, he began scraping away the explosive which had moulded itself around the photocell's wires. Chunks of the wax-like explosive flaked away until eventually the wires were all exposed. Dropping the big knife, he attached his circuit-detector box to the copper strands and used his chin to switch it to 'Run'.

Once again, the box's quartz screen told him exactly which wires to cut. Feeling sick and dizzier still, he selected the two wires and cut each of them in two places. But the world was starting to spin and Felix could see blackness at the fringes of his vision. *Hold it together.* Still clinging to his girder like a sloth to a branch, he repeated the procedure on the mercury tilt-switch. Eyes flickering, he again severed the link, separating the bomb's brain from its monstrous body.

But still the device wasn't truly dead.

Willing himself to hold on just a little longer, Felix reached into the case and his hand closed on the plastic explosive moulded around the sphere of plutonium. He started pulling away the detonators as carefully as he could.

'Felix,' Zane shouted, 'what the hell are you doing?'

'It's not exactly textbook,' Felix admitted weakly. 'But this cut-price plutonium will be giving out enough heat to maybe set off the primary explosive, which would set off the C4 around it and start fission.' He let the dets slip from his grasp. 'Now, you really want to get this device properly shielded before you find someone to take it apart.'

'I do?'

'You do,' Felix agreed, starting to slip from the girder. ''Cause, me, I think I'm going to pass out . . .'

'Felix!' Zane ran over and just managed to catch him as he fell. 'Jesus, man, look at the state of you. Have you really beaten the nuke? Are we good?'

'You're good.' Felix's eyes began to flicker shut. 'But me – I'm bloody brilliant . . .'

And the world went truly dark again. But it was the most warm and peaceful darkness that Felix had known for a long, long time.

COUNTDOWN: RESET

Felix opened his eyes. Everything was white. Crisp, flaw-
less stretches of it. He wondered for a moment if he'd
died and this was some angel-bright heaven. Then he
moved his head a little way and found he'd been looking
up close at a starched duvet. Groggily he realized he was
in a hospital room. A jug of water stood on the table
beside him. A vase of tulips waited on the windowsill, the
flowers' long red faces bright against the blue sky.

He tried to push himself up in bed, and straight away
found his hand was in a cast, with an intravenous drip
poking out from the back of his wrist. At the same time,
his right thigh burned as his dressed wound rubbed
against the duvet cover, and he gasped with pain.

'You called?' The door to his right swung open to
reveal Zane, a laptop tucked under one arm and a half-
eaten bunch of grapes in the other. 'Welcome back to the

land of the living, Felix . . . or of the walking wounded, in any case. You're in a private hospital in central London.'

Felix tried to smile through a wave of nausea. 'The bomb . . . ?'

'In pieces,' Zane confirmed. 'But you've been put back together, right down to your Minos chain. Can't have you going off the radar again, can we?'

'I feel dizzy.'

'Probably the anaesthetic. Or the blood transfusion.'

Felix touched the pendant at his neck and looked again at the cast on his other hand. 'What about this?'

'Three hours in surgery ought to have done some good.' Zane put down the grapes and opened the laptop. 'The breaks were pretty clean, and the surgeon was the best. He's confident that with an intensive course of physio you'll be pretty much as good as new within three to four weeks.'

Felix let his head sink back onto his pillow with relief. 'Does the surgeon know how I got the injuries?'

'Does he hell. I said you'd been mugged for your lunch money.' He smiled. 'The government and GI5 are keeping all knowledge of Kanska's conspiracy under wraps. Don't want anything to dent the country's morale on the golden day she gets back her busiest airport.'

'Then they'll never know how close they came to . . .'

'Better that way,' Zane insisted. 'But GI5 knows, Felix. Which means you and I get to keep our jobs – Minos won't be closing down any time soon.'

'That's great. I think.' Felix smiled back at him. 'How

did you find me, anyway? Did the Girl – I mean, the tera-head I talked to—'

'She worked out that something wasn't on the level,' Zane assured him, munching on the grapes as he tapped at the laptop. 'But there wasn't a whole lot to go on – until we got sent fifty gigabytes of long-haul trafficking data.'

'The cloned network data I took from Blackmoon?' Felix blinked. 'But the drive was in my pocket, I lost it. How the hell did you—'

'Why not ask your taxi driver?' Zane suggested, turning round the laptop to face him.

Felix sat up straight with shock – and quickly wished he hadn't as his leg burned again. 'Abdul!' he cried, wincing with pain.

'You aren't pleased to see me?' Abdul teased from the webcam window. 'What, you're too much the big man now to bother with the man who saved your sorry butt?'

'How did you—'

Abdul beamed. 'I told you I would have a good drive, didn't I? I meant the portable *hard* drive. When you were drugged and stumbled, I held you steady, yes? Well, while I helped you, I helped myself to that little gadget. Took it from your pocket.'

'You're clever.'

'Had I been truly clever, I'd have taken your wallet too at the same time,' Abdul lamented. 'Kanska's friends held me prisoner for three days. Since I could only send and receive messages to Minos at my cousin's net café, they had to hold him prisoner too. For three days we were helpless. Helpless!' His eyes shone with pride as he recounted his tale. 'Only not quite, for in the end I was able to unlock my cousin's menagerie of snakes and spiders – a most hungry and irate menagerie – and we bravely overpowered our enemies.'

Felix grinned. 'You couldn't make it up. But I guess together we fixed Kanska.' He looked at Zane. 'What gave him away in the end?'

'These days, for security, every port and airport has been fitted with Automated Numberplate Recognition cameras to monitor traffic-flow in and out.' Zane ate another handful of grapes. 'We had a partial number-plate, IDed from Henri's "insurance" footage, and the dates that the footage was taken. By cross-referencing that against both the dates of Blackmoon's trans-European deliveries and the numberplates showing up on the Port Authorities' systems, we narrowed down the hunt for your truck to a handful of suspect vehicles and waited to see which one would turn up.'

'Sounds a bigger nightmare than what I went through,' Felix joked.

'Tera-heads love that stuff.' Zane grinned as he plucked several more of the choicest grapes from the bunch. 'Meantime, we checked registrations of vehicles in and out of every airport car park in the UK. And you know when firms buy a fleet new from the same supplier the numberplates are similar?'

Abdul joined in the conversation from the laptop, wide-eyed. 'You found one which matched?'

'The UK plates on that truck carrying Felix and Kanska

were just a couple of digits up from two heavy goods vehicles belonging to one of the construction firms at New Heathrow,' Zane explained. 'By then, the truck's plates had been snapped at Southampton but we didn't know where it was headed . . . till we checked out the firm's property holdings and found that warehouse in Stanwell had been built just six months ago – the only site they owned in the vicinity of New Heathrow. But we had no way of knowing if Felix was still on that truck or had been taken elsewhere.'

'Just glad I survived the friendly fire,' said Felix with feeling. 'Glad I survived at all.'

'You've got your friend the Girl to thank for it,' Zane informed him. 'She came up with the strategy and over-saw it herself.'

'D'you know her name?' Felix asked.

Zane shrugged evasively. 'I know a lot of girls' names.'

'Well, I hope you haven't forgotten mine!' The South African accent boomed down the corridor outside like a foghorn.

Felix grinned. 'Hannah!'

'Hey, my bru!' She came in through the door on crutches, a white towelling dressing gown flapping around her ankles. 'You look good with dark hair. You doing OK?'

'Surviving, just. How are you feeling?'

'Hundreds,' she said. 'You don't get rid of me that easily.'

'But I will let you be rid of me, Junior,' Adbul called from the laptop. 'I still have to help round up some long-legged friends. Congratulations on your new airport, and may you use it to come to Irbil one day . . . and bring a fat wallet.'

'I'll be seeing you, Abdul,' Felix told him. 'Or should I say, Big Man?'

Abdul grinned, touched his heart and cut the connection.

'Big Man?' Hannah jokily frowned. 'Just how close did you two get out there?'

Felix tutted. 'You've got a one-track mind.'

'And this country's got a one-track media,' Hannah shot back. 'Nothing but New Heathrow's opening on the box. Different VIP gassing on every channel.' She smiled, the playful edge gone from her voice now. 'You did it, Felix. That was . . . well. Nice work.'

He smiled back. 'You did tell me not to let the bad guys win.'

'Oh, pur-leeeze,' Zane objected, plucking the last of the grapes from the skeleton of stalks. 'Listen, I'll catch you later.'

'Hey, what about my grapes?'

'They were delicious, man.'

'Zane?' Felix nodded. 'Thanks for the cavalry bit. I owe you.'

'Damn right you do.' He paused in the doorway, eyes glinting as he smiled. 'And don't you worry. I aim to collect . . .'

The door clicked shut.

Hannah looked a little awkward now, and hardened her voice. 'Ja, well, next time can you at least try and save the world using both hands?' She perched on the edge of his bed. 'No one likes a smartarse.'

Felix eyed his cast ruefully. 'Both hands. Right. I'll try and remember that. And you know, I'll always remember something else you told me.'

'Which was?'

'You can save lives and have one yourself.' He looked at her. 'I nearly died today. But I didn't.' He grinned. 'And right now, I think I want to snog someone.'

'Oh?' Hannah turned away. 'Well, not interested.' Then she looked back over her shoulder and grinned. 'Much. The dark hair is hot . . .'

She leaned in and gave him a big smacker on the lips. It meant little in the big scheme of things beyond a simple sharing of happiness. But as their lips broke apart, Felix found that he finally felt a thump of warmth in his chest, something more than fear or determination or grief for times now lost; all the possibilities that popped into being when you stopped fearing the future or mourning the past, and just freefalled through the moment.

'Who knows if they'll pair us together again, bru. But I kind of hope they do.' Hannah looked at him thoughtfully. 'Be careful out there, Felix. You've been lucky. But no one's luck lasts for ever.'

Felix shrugged. 'So we do what we can, while we can.'

'Damn right.' She got back up with her crutches. 'I'll visit you again.'

'Do that,' he said. 'And take it easy, yeah?'

'Easy. Right. I live to take it easy.' He watched Hannah limp doggedly to the door.

Like her, he was hurting, injured. Damaged.

And like her, he knew he would pull through and get out there for Minos again.

What else was there to do?

Late that night, Felix flouted the rules. He picked up his saline drip-bag, dodged past the nurses and sneaked out onto the concrete roof of the hospital to look out over the city at night; the heavy-duty landmarks of the capital nestling amid the skyscrapers, lighting the horizon. But for better or worse, it was London, and he loved it. A light rain had fallen, and the high-rise landscape felt vibrant and alive.

His phone rang in his dressing-gown pocket. He placed the IV bag on a chimney-stack and pulled it out. The screen read: NUMBER WITHHELD. Intrigued, Felix accepted the call.

'How's the view?' asked the Girl.

Felix smiled as a plane soared slowly through the sky overhead, lights winking as it banked away. 'Sweet.'

'It's there because of you.'

'And because of you. If you hadn't figured out the way to track that truck and steered the cavalry to the warehouse . . .'

'OK. I guess we worked together quite well on this one.'

Felix nodded, enjoying the cool night breeze on his face. 'We did.'

'Your father would be proud of you.'

'I know,' he said. 'Funny, I always used to imagine that

one day I'd be a big hero, that some day I would defuse the mother of all IEDs and look down and say . . . I don't know. "That was for you, Dad," or something.'

'If life was a big Hollywood film, you would've done.'

'Yeah. But now I know I didn't do it for Dad, or to avenge all those who died in Day Zero.' Felix stared out over the neon-washed skyline. 'I did it for the ones who lived . . . like me.'

The distant traffic droned its urban lullaby.

'You know, it's against the rules to call you when I'm on leave,' the Girl announced suddenly. 'I could get us both into trouble.'

'You could?'

'Yes.' She hesitated. 'You know, there are times when I don't really know what I'm doing.'

'Sounds familiar,' Felix murmured. 'Hey . . . If you're on leave, and I'm off the active list for a bit, can you come and visit?'

She paused. 'That wouldn't be acceptable.'

'Stuff acceptable,' Felix retorted. 'If this job gives us a split-second life span, I'm aiming to get full value out of every instant.'

'Fighting talk.'

'I used to box at school.'

'That's not on your file.'

'Maybe I made it up. Or maybe there's a lot about me that's not on my file.'

'You think so?' The Girl fell silent for a few seconds. 'I should go,' she said finally. 'I'm glad it's a clear night for you tonight. Keep enjoying the view. But perhaps you should stand a little further from the edge?'

'Wow,' Felix marvelled. 'Those Minos trackers are really mega-accurate.'

'Goodnight, Felix. Get well soon.'

'Copy that,' Felix murmured, as the Girl rang off. He took a deep breath of dirty, gorgeous London air. He was sore and shattered. He ought to turn in. He could sleep in a safe bed. It was all good.

He would do that soon. But for now there was the view. And the feeling inside that he was king of the world.

Felix smiled to himself. A buzz like this could be habit-forming . . .

In the street opposite the hospital, the Girl stood away from the phone kiosk and looked up at Felix's silhouette high above on the building's edge. He looked as though he was making ready to launch himself into the darkness.

'Tonight you must feel you can fly,' the Girl whispered.

If only she didn't know what was coming.

I hope you stay flying, Felix. I hope you never fall.

She turned and walked away along the empty street. A stiffening wind that spoke of autumn stirred the trees, and sent dirt and litter snapping at her heels. She glanced back at the top of the hospital building and saw that Felix was still there.

Watching and waiting for the next time.

GLOSSARY

Types of IED – Improvised Explosive Device

CWIED: A command wire IED that uses an electrical firing cable so that the person activating the device has complete control

RCIED: The trigger for this Radio-Controlled IED is controlled by a radio link so that it can be operated at a distance

Cell phone RCIED: A radio-controlled IED that uses a mobile phone connected to an electrical firing circuit. Often the phone receiving a signal is enough to initiate the firing circuit

Petrol bomb: A hand-thrown device that contains a flammable substance. It functions on impact

Pipe bomb: A crude IED that contains either a high or low explosive in a metal tube that is sealed at both ends. The device is normally activated by a timer

Secondary device: The purpose of these devices is to target those involved in responding to an IED incident

Suicide IED: Explosive devices that are delivered to the target and activated by a human. The bomber deliberately loses his life

VBIED: A Vehicle Born IED that has some kind of vehicle as part of its construction. The vehicle hides the parts of the IED and can make an explosion more dangerous

VOIED: Victim Operated – these function following contact with a victim and are also known as booby traps. They are operated by movement

AK47:	Selective fire assault rifle
AMS:	Acute Mountain Sickness
ARS:	Acute Radiation Syndrome
ATLAS:	Anti-Terrorist Logistics Assessment Service
Bergen:	Pack carried by British forces
Black Ops:	A covert operation
Coalition:	A unified group involved in a military operation
CS gas:	Tear gas
DZ:	Day Zero
ECM jammer:	Electronic counter-measure jammer blocks communication wavelengths to prevent signals getting through
Fast-roping:	Technique for descending a thick rope quickly
GI5:	Allied Secret Intelligence Service
GPS:	Global Positioning System
Guerrillas:	Small mobile groups of combatants using ambush techniques such as raids to combat a larger, less mobile force.
Handrail:	The orienteering technique of following long, narrow features without a compass
IED:	Improvised explosive device
LDR:	Light dependent resistor
LED:	Light emitting diode
MI6:	UK's Secret Intelligence Service
Minos Chapter:	Secret wing of ATLAS made up of teenage agents
MO:	Latin, *Modus Operandi* – meaning 'method of operation'

M3:	Submachine gun in service 1942-1992
M4 Carbine:	Shorter and lighter version of the M16 A2 – assault rifle
M16:	Primary infantry rifle of the US military
Navy SEAL:	Member of the US Navy, Sea, Air and Land Forces
PackBot:	A military robot
PE4:	British plastic explosive
Pelican case:	Airtight and watertight plastic container
Pentanex 8:	Chemical explosive more powerful than TNT
PIR:	Passive infrared sensor, detects movement or presence by infrared emissions
PKK:	Kurdistan Workers' Party, terrorist organization
PMN-2:	Type of anti-personnel mine
RPG:	Rocket-propelled grenade
S10:	Protective gas mask, respirator
SAS:	Special Air Service
SIG 229:	Automatic pistol
TA:	Territorial Army
TEDAC:	Technical Explosive Device Exploitation Centre
Tetryl:	A sensitive explosive compound
Thuraya:	Regional satellite phone provider
TNT:	Trinitrotoluene (standard military high explosive)
TPU:	Timing and power unit
XPAK:	Explosives detection device
747:	Boeing 747, large aircraft

ABOUT THE AUTHORS

STEVE COLE is the author of the huge, best-selling *Astrosaurs* and *Cows In Action* series and has now written thirty-six books published by RHCB. *Tripwire* is his first novel with Chris Hunter and there are more titles in the series to come.

Steve has also written many titles for other publishers, including several *Doctor Who* novels, which have become UK bestsellers. He has also been the editor of fiction and nonfiction book titles.

Steve lives in Buckinghamshire, with his wife and two children. You can find out more about him at www.stevecolebooks.co.uk

Tripwire is Major **CHRIS HUNTER**'s first book for younger readers. He joined the British army in 1989 at the age of sixteen. He was commissioned from Sandhurst at twenty-one and later qualified as a counter-terrorist bomb-disposal operator, serving with many units in dangerous situations across the world. He was awarded the Queen's Gallantry Medal for his work in Iraq.

Chris now lives in London and works as an IED consultant. You can find out more about him at www.tripwirebooks.co.uk

THE FIGHT AGAINST THE
TERRORISTS IS NOT OVER

FELIX HAS WORK TO DO . . .

TRIPWIRE

BOOK 2

COMING 2011